CONTENTS

For Maria Alexander and Brett Shefter,
With love.

INTRODUCTION

I don't write horror stories.
They write me.

—*David Gerrold*

SKINFLOWERS

On Wednesday, there were bristly patches on the backs of his hands. They looked like a field of tiny white goose bumps and gave his skin a sandpapery feeling. He didn't like it; he was in the habit of rubbing the back of one hand against his cheek. He hadn't shaved this morning and the roughness of his hand matched the roughness of his face. It disturbed him.

—and yet, somehow, the scratchiness of the sensation was intriguing. As he rubbed his bristly hands thoughtfully, he decided not to shave at all.

On Thursday, the bumps on his hands were stiffer. They seemed to be growing into tiny little spines. Although they were firm, they weren't rigid. They stood away from the skin, but they could be pressed back into it without any feeling. They weren't painful, so he felt a curious lack of distress about them.

Friday, the first of the flowers appeared.

The spines were noticeably longer by then. Most had tiny swellings at their ends. One or two of the swellings had begun to open up into little cuplike shapes, but it wasn't until Saturday that there were recognizable clusters on each hand.

The blossoms were carefully shaped cusps, one at the end of each pale stem; a fleshy convex lens. They were as white as bloodless skin.

Saturday was when he first began to be aware of them—really aware. And curious. Why was there a field of delicate flowers on the back of each of his hands and wrists? Turning on the high intensity lamp over his desk, he examined them carefully.

The stems were less than a quarter inch in length. They were flexible and seemed to be extensions of the skin itself. The blossoms were shaped like dichondra, each a single white cusp. He felt no sensation from then at all.

Some kind of growth, perhaps—? He tried cutting them off with a razor. The smaller ones came off easily, but the larger flowers tugged and resisted as if their stems were beginning to become cartilaginous. The scissors worked better than the razor, but it left uneven and bristly stubs. They felt as scraggly as a three-day beard and they looked even worse. Besides, cutting the flowers gave him an uneasy feeling—as if he were amputating part of himself. So he stopped with his left hand. He didn't cut the flowers from his right one.

He didn't go out on Saturday—except once to the grocery store. The gloves he wore were uncomfortable. They pressed the flowers into his skin and they seemed to irritate the rough patches of spines. He was glad to get them off when he got home again.

He rubbed at the flowers on his right hand as if to restore their circulation and make them stand up again. It wasn't necessary. They moved easily at his touch. But there was no sensation at all from them, nor from the patches of spines and bumps that were extending up the back of his forearm.

The skin beneath still had sensation though, and the feel of the flowers between his fingers and his skin was most peculiar—like moist warm leaves. Like soft dry noodles. He almost enjoyed the way they felt as he ran his fingers through them. The sensation was as interesting as the hole left behind by a tooth freshly pulled out.

On Sunday, there were more of the flowers. On his right arm, they extended across his wrist and fresh buds were appearing on his forearm. On his left, where he had cut them, they were already beginning to grow back. Many of the spines had already opened their buds. For some reason, that pleased him. He was afraid he might have damaged them when he cut them, and he was curious to see just how far they would spread and how large they would grow.

The newer buds on his arms were still very tiny, but the oldest ones were almost as big across as the nail of his little finger. The close, edge-to-edge pattern they formed was fascinating to look at; they were a clustered field of pink-white cups. They were beginning to take on color.

As he sat in his chair and stroked the back of his hand across his neck and cheek he became aware of their odor. It wasn't an unpleasant odor— it was kind of sweet-sour and fleshy, almost-like the familiar smell of old ages but not quite. It was the smell of skin, the fragrance of flesh. What gave it its hint of pungency though, was its almost total lack of musk. The odor was more flowery than human.

Idly, he wondered what they were, these skinflowers. Abnormal growths of some kind? Or a new development of his body, one that could have been expected? If they were natural, what should he do about them? Were they like hair —to be groomed and admired? Or were they blemishes, like unsightly warts?

And if they were unnatural, what then? Maybe they were parasites— tiny plants or animals that had imbedded themselves in his skin and were actively reproducing like real flowers in fertile soil. No. He doubted that. These flowers were too much like flesh, they were too much a part of him.

Maybe they were some kind of disease -like a tumor. But he doubted that too. They weren't painful, and he'd never heard of any disease where the skin broke out in flowers.

No, they must be some kind of natural development. As he examined them curiously, he noticed that the flowers seemed to be replacing the hair on his hands and arms. The skin beneath the stems was pink and fresh, completely hairless. Parasites wouldn't do that, would they? Neither would a disease. These skinflowers were probably a different kind of hair, perhaps their stems were just a different kind of hair follicle.

Except that he had heard somewhere that hair wasn't alive; it was protein produced by the follicle and the actual shaft was dead material. These skinflowers were obviously alive. The ones he had cut on Saturday were quickly replacing themselves.

Well, perhaps his hair follicles had changed somehow. It wasn't inconceivable. He stroked his arms fretfully, and the sensation comforted him. The feel of the tiny cups of flesh as they pulled and rolled across his skin was...interesting.

On Monday, he decided to wear a short-sleeved shirt around the house. He didn't want to cover up his flowers. He enjoyed looking at them. He enjoyed touching them and stroking his cheek with the back of his hand and arm. He was fascinated by their scent. They were almost up to his elbows by now.

On the older flowers, the stems had turned pink and the cups were beginning to take on a more definite color. The shading was delicate, from rose at the center of each blossom, fading almost to white at the edge. The rim of each cup retained its hint of bloodlessness, outlining each flower with a pale halo.

He spent long hours just studying them, touching them and caressing them, rubbing them against his cheek, rubbing them against his nose and mouth. He found himself sucking meditatively on the blossoms, almost—but not quite—nipping them off with his teeth. He would bury his nostrils in them and luxuriate in their fleshy smell.

When he discovered the rough patches on his shoulders, as well as at the base of his spine, he was delighted. That meant the flowers were not to be limited to just his hands and arms. He longed for their spread—they produced a weightless, almost floating sensation in his arms and he ached to immerse his whole body in the sensation.

In the next few days, the patches on his shoulders and back grew into spines and then into clumps of pink dichondra. The cups were larger here, more developed. And they seemed more rugged than the blossoms that covered his arms, which were almost all the way up to his shoulders now. The flowers spread quickly across his shoulder blades, like a mantle, and down his back. The first patches of roughness appeared on his legs.

The smell was stronger by now, much stronger. He seemed to move in a cloud of it, but he wasn't always conscious of the odor. His nose had grown used to it, and it was only when he moved suddenly that he was aware of his smell.

The scent had the sweetness of decay, but without the cloying pungency of rot. It was a flowery-sour smell—like roses, too many and too ripe. He liked it though. It was a part of him.

Sleeping was developing into a problem though. He didn't like seeing the flowers crushed each morning. They weren't hurt by the pressure of his body-weight on them for a night, but it usually took an hour or so for them to resume their resiliency. In addition, the stems were beginning to develop a sensitivity of their own. If pressed the wrong way for too long, they began to ache like hair that has been brushed against its natural direction and held that way.

He took to sleeping on his stomach with only a single sheet instead of a blanket. He wasn't masturbating any more either. He was too intrigued with the taste and texture of his flowers. And the overall sensation of lightness. He moved in a trance-like daze. He floated. Usually, he would fall asleep with his nose and mouth pressed against the back of his right forearm where the flowers were thickest.

The flowers spread to his feet, covering all but the soles and the toenails. They clustered across the top of the arch and two or three even grew out of each toe. lie stopped wearing shoes snd socks. And when the flowers covered his legs he stopped wearing pants. He felt like he was immersed in sweet oil.

They appeared on his neck and soon after even on the back of his head where they looked like tiny ears. They began to replace his hair. A rough patch appeared on his belly and grew downward. These blossoms were slightly darker, slightly redder than the rest, especially where his pubic hair had been. His penis was surrounded by a forest of curlicue stems and crimson cusps. By then, most of his chest was covered too.

Oddly, the flowers did not appear on his face. They curled down his ears, like scarlet sideburns, and they crept around his neck like a flaming beard. They capped his brow like a thicket of red ringlets, and they even replaced his eyebrows with miniscule blossoms, but they did not appear on his cheeks and forehead.

By the time his body was completely covered by the flowers, he was no longer wearing any clothes at all. He was swimming in cold euphoria. It was rosy and blurred, He no longer had any trouble sleeping now; the flowers had grown stronger and more resilient to his weight. The sensitivity had been only a temporary phase.

He found that direct sunlight was too strong for him now, and he spent more and more time indoors. He only liked being outside during the night. He began sleeping later each day and staying awake longer into the dark, until after a while he had reversed his normal habits.

The colors of the flowers deepened now, grew richer. Across his back, they shaded from deep brown to pale yellow, with here and there a hint of red or purple. On his chest and stomach, the colors were lighter, but there were patterns of shades, darker where there had been hair, lighter where there had been none. His arms and legs repeated this coloring, the insides of the limbs being paler, the outsides being darker.

And the smell of the flowers was rank now, almost overpowering. He didn't notice—and even if he had, he wouldn't have minded. He liked them. Hle liked their feel and their fragrance. He liked to lose himself in their curls.

He stood out in the yard each night and bared himself to the sky. He opened his flowers and his pores, and let them suck in the blackness, let them ripple the coolness all through his body.

There was no moon, and even the stars were diminished. There was only darkness, cold enveloping darkness. He stretched his arms out to it.

His state was trancelike, disembodied. He floated in the night and waited for the harvesters to come.

—and when they did, they plucked the flowers from him with a scream. They stripped the skin from his body and left him twitching and raw, jerking like something that had been flayed.

*

In the morning, she found bristly patches on the backs of her hands...

REX

"Daddy! The tyrannosaur is loose again! He jumped the fence."

Jonathan Filltree replied with a single word, one which he didn't want his eight-year-old daughter to hear. He punched the *save* key on his keyboard, kicked back his chair and headed toward the basement stairs with obvious annoyance. He resented these constant interruptions in the flow of his work.

"Hurry, Daddy!" Jill shouted again from the basement door. "He's chasing the stegosaurs! He's gonna get Steggy!"

"I warned you this was going to happen—" Filltree said angrily, grabbing the long-handled net off the wall. "No! Wait here," he snapped.

"That's not fair!" cried Jill, following him down the bare wooden stairs. "I didn't know he was going to get this big!"

"He's a meat-eater. The stegosaurs and the apatosaurs and all the others look like lunch to him. Get back upstairs, Jill!"

Filltree stopped at the bottom and looked slowly around the basement that his wife had demanded he convert into a miniature dinosaur kingdom for their spoiled daughter. Hot yellow lights bathed the cellar in a prehistoric ambience. A carboniferous smell permeated everything. He wrinkled his nose in distaste. For some reason, it was worse than usual.

The immediate problem was obvious. Most of the six-inch stegosaurs had retreated to the high slopes that butted up against the north wall, where they milled about nervously. Their bright yellow and orange colors made them easy to see. Quickly, he counted. All three of the calves and their mother were okay; so were the other two females; but they were all cheeping in distress. He spotted Fred and Cyril, but Steggy was not with the others. The two remaining males were emitting rasping peeps of agitation; and they kept making angry charging motions downslope.

Filltree followed the direction of their agitation. "Damn!" he said, spotting the two-foot-high tyrannosaur. Rex was ripping long strips of flesh off the side of the fallen Steggy and gulping them hungrily down. Already he was streaked with blood. His long tail lashed furiously in the air, acting as a counterweight as he bent to his kill. He ripped and tore, then rose up on his haunches, glancing around quickly and checking for danger with sharp bird-like motions. He jerked his head upward to gulp the latest bloody gobbet deeper into his mouth, then gulped a second time to swallow it. He grunted and roared, then lowered his whole body forward to again bury his muzzle deep in gore.

"Oh, Daddy! He's killed Steggy!"

"I told you to wait upstairs! A tyrannosaur can be dangerous when he's feeding!"

"But he's killed Steggy—!"

"Well, I'm sorry. There's nothing to do now but wait until he finishes and goes torpid." Filltree put the net down, leaning it against the edge of the table. The entire room was filled with an elaborate waist-high miniature landscape, through which an improbable mix of Cretaceous and Jurassic creatures prowled. The glass fences at the edges of the tables were all at least 36 inches high, and mildly electrified to keep the various creatures safely enclosed. Until they'd added Rex to the huge terrarium, they'd had one of the finest collections in Westchester, with over a hundred dinos prowling through the miniature forests. And every spring, the new births among the various herbivores usually added five to ten adorable little calves to their herds.

Now, the ranks of their menagerie had been reduced to only a few light-footed stegosaurs, some lumbering apatosaurs, two armored anky-losaurs, the belligerent triceratops herd, and the chirruping hadrosaurs. Most of those had survived only because their favorite grazing grounds were at one end of the huge U-shaped environment, and Rex's corral was all the way around at the opposite end. Rex wandered around the herbivore grounds only until he found something to attack. Like most of the mini-dinos, Rex didn't have a lot of gray matter to work with; he almost always attacked the first moving object he saw. In the six months since his installation in what Filltree had once believed was a secure corral, Rex had more than decimated the population of the Pleasant Avenue Dinosaur Zoo. He was now escaping regularly once or twice a week.

Slowly, Filltree worked his way around the table to the corral, examining all the fences carefully to see where and how the tyrannosaur might have broken through the barriers. He had thought for sure that the 30-inch-high rock-surfaced polyfoam bricks he had installed last week would finally keep the carnivore from escaping again to terrorize the more placid herbivores. Obviously, he had been wrong.

Filltree frowned as he studied the thick blockade. It had not been broken through in any place, nor had the tyrant-lizard dug a hole underneath it. The rocks were not chewed, but they were badly scratched in several places. Filltree leaned across the table for a closer look. "Mm," he said.

"What is it, Daddy? Tell me!" Jill demanded impatiently.

He pointed. The sides and tops of the bricks were sharply gouged. Rex had leapt up onto the top of the wall, surveyed the opposite side, and leapt down to feed. Judging from the numerous marks carved into the surface, today's outing was clearly not the first. "See. Rex can leap the fence. And that probably explains the mysterious disappearance of the last coelophysis too. This is getting ridiculous, Jill. I can't afford this anymore. We're going to have to find a new home for Rex."

"Daddy, no!" Jill became immediately belligerent. "Rexy is part of our family!"

"Rexy is eating up all the other dinosaurs, Jill. That's not very family-like."

"We can buy new ones."

"No, we can't. Dinosaurs cost money, and I'm not buying any new animals until we get rid of him. I'm sorry, kiddo; but I told you this wasn't going to work."

"Daddy, pleeeaase—! Rexy is my favorite!"

Jonathan Filltree took his daughter by the hand and led her back around to where Rexy was still gorging himself on the now unrecognizable remains of the much smaller stegosaur. "Look, Jill. This is going to keep happening, sweetheart. Rexy is getting too big for us to keep. It's all that fresh beef that you and Mommy keep feeding him. Remember what the dinosaur-doctor said? It accelerates his growth. But you didn't listen. Now, none of the other dinosaurs can escape him or even fight back. It isn't fair to them. And it isn't fair to Rexy either to keep him in a place where he won't be happy."

That last part was a complete fabrication on his part, and Filltree knew it even as he spoke it. If Rexy was capable of happiness, then he was probably very happy to be living in a place where he was the only carnivore and all of the prey animals were too small to resist his attacks. According to the genetic specifications, however, Rexy and the other mini-dinosaurs would have had to borrow the synapses necessary to complete a thought. Calling them stupid would have been a compliment.

"But—but, you can't! He'll miss me!"

Filltree sighed with exhaustion. He already knew how this argument was going to end. Jill would go to Mommy, and Mommy would promise to talk to Daddy. And then Mommy would sulk for two weeks because Daddy wanted her to break a promise to their darling little girl. And finally, he'd give in just to get a little peace and quiet again so he could get some work done. But he had to try anyway. He dropped to one knee in front of his daughter and put his hands on her shoulders. "We'll find a good place for him, Jilly, I promise." And even as he said it, he knew it was a promise he'd never be able to keep.

He knew he wouldn't be able to sell Rex. He'd seen the ads in the Recycler. There was no market for tyrant-lizards anymore—of any size. And Rexy was more than two feet high, and rapidly approaching the legal maximum of 36 inches. Rexy required ten pounds of fresh meat a week; he'd only eat dry kibble when the alternative was starvation. They still had half a bag of Purina Dinosaur Chow left from when they'd first bought him. The dinosaur would go for almost a week without eating before he'd touch the stuff, and even then he'd only pick at it.

Nor did Filltree think he'd even be able to give the creature away. The zoo didn't want any more tyrannosaurs, of *any* size. They were expensive to feed and they already had over a hundred of the little monsters, spitting and hissing and roaring—and occasionally devouring the smaller of their brethren.

At one time it had been fashionable to own your own miniature T. Rex; but the fad had passed, the tyrant-lizards had literally outgrown their welcome, the price of meat had risen again (due to the Brazilian droughts), and a lot of people—wearying of the smells and the bother—had finally dropped their pets off at the zoo or turned them over to the animal shelters. Because they were protected under the Artificial Species

Act, the cost of putting a mini-dino down was almost prohibitive. Some thoughtless individuals had tried abandoning their hungry dinosaurs in the wild, not realizing that the animals were genetically traceable. The fines, according to the newspaper reports, had been astonishing.

"I promise you, Jilly, we'll find a place for Rexy where he'll be happy and we can visit him every week, okay?"

Jill shook his hands off, folded her arms in front of her, and turned away. "No!" she decided. "You're not giving Rexy away! He's my dinosaur. I picked him out and you said I could have him."

Filltree gave up. He turned back to the diorama. Rexy had stopped gorging himself and was now standing torpidly near his kill. Filltree grabbed the metal-mesh net and quickly brought it down over the dinosaur. Rexy struggled in the mesh, but not wildly. Filltree had learned a long time ago to wait until the tyrant-king had finished eating before trying to return him to his corral. He swung the net across the table, taking care to hold the dinosaur well away from him and as high as he could. Jill tried to reach up to grab the handle of the net, and instinctively he yanked it up out of her reach—but for just a moment, the temptation flickered across his mind to let her actually grab Rexy. Then he'd see how much she loved the little monster.

But…if he did, he'd never hear the end of it, he knew that—and besides, there was the danger that the mini-dino might actually do some serious damage. So he ignored Jill's yelps of protest and returned Rexy to his own kingdom. Temporarily at least. Then he went back and scooped up the bloody remains of poor Steggy and wordlessly tossed that into Rexy's domain as well.

"Aren't we going to have a funeral for Steggy?"

"No, we're not. We've had enough funerals. All it does is annoy the tyrannosaur. Let Rexy have his meal. It'll keep him from jumping the fence for another week or two. Maybe. I hope. Come on. I told you to stay upstairs. And you didn't listen. Just for that, no dessert—"

"I'm gonna tell Mommy!"

"You do that," he sighed tiredly, following her up the stairs—realizing that of all the animals in the house, the one he resented most was the one who was supposed to know better. She was eight and a half years old—at that age, they were supposed to be almost human, weren't they? He felt exhausted. He knew he wasn't going to get any more work done today. Not after Jilly finished crying to Mommy about Daddy threatening to get rid of poor little Rexy. "Rexy didn't mean to do anything wrong," he mimed to himself. "He was hungry because Daddy forgot to feed him last night."

Filltree both hated and envied Rexy. Jill gave all her attention and affection to the dinosaur, speaking to Daddy only when demanding something else for her collection of creatures. And Mommy was another one—she paid more attention to preparing the little tyrant's meals than to his. The dinosaur got fresh beef or lamb three times a week. He got soy-burgers.

For a long while, he'd been considering the idea of a separation— maybe even a divorce. He'd even gone so far as to log onto the Legal-Net website and crunch the numbers on their divorce-judgment simulator. Although Legal-Net refused to guarantee the accuracy of its legal software, lest they expose themselves to numerous lawsuits, the divorce-judgment simulator used the same Judicial Engine as the Federal Divorce Court, and was unofficially rated at ninety percent accuracy in its extrapolations.

All he wanted was a tiny little condo somewhere up in the hills, a place where he could sit and work and stare out the window in peace without having to think about tyrants, either the two-foot kind or the three-foot kind. Tyrant lizards, tyrant children—the only difference he could see was that the tyrant lizard only ate your heart out once and then it was done.

According to the simulator, he could afford the condo; that wasn't the problem. *Unfortunately*, also according to Legal-Net's Judicial Engine he could not afford the simultaneous maintenance of Joyce and Jill. The simulator gave him several options, none of them workable from his point of view. A divorce would give him freedom, but it would be prohibitively expensive. A separation would give him peace and quiet, but it wouldn't give him freedom—and he'd still have to keep up the payments on Joyce and Jill's various expensive habits.

Grunting in annoyance, he pulled the heavy carry cage out of the garage and lugged it awkwardly back down the basement stairs. Jilly followed him the whole way, whining and crying. He slipped easily into his robot-daddy mode, disconnecting his emotions and refusing to respond to even her most provocative assaults. "I don't love you anymore. You promised me. I'm not your daughter anymore. I'm gonna tell Mommy. I don't like you. You can go to hell."

"Don't tempt me. I might enjoy the change," he muttered in reply to the last remark.

Back downstairs, Filltree discovered that Rexy had not only finished his meal; he was already standing on top of the rock barrier again, lashing his tail furiously and studying the realm beyond. He looked like he was preparing to return to his hunting. At the opposite end of the room, the remaining stegosaurs were mooing agitatedly.

Rexy spotted them then. He turned sharply to glare across the intervening distance, cocking his head with birdlike motions to study them first with one baleful black eye, then the other. Perhaps it was just the shape of his head, but his expression seemed ominous and calculating. The creature's eyes were filled with hatred for the soft pink mammals who restricted him, as well as insatiable hunger for the taste of human flesh. Filltree wondered why he'd ever wanted a tyrannosaur in the first place. Rexy hissed in defiance, arching his neck forward and opening his mouth wide to reveal ranks of knife-sharp little teeth.

Filltree frowned. Was it his imagination or had the little tyrannosaur grown another six inches in the last six minutes? The creature seemed a lot bigger than he remembered him being. Of course, he'd been so angry at the little monster that he hadn't really looked at him closely for a while.

"He's awfully big. Have you been feeding him again?" he demanded of his daughter.

"No!" Jill said, indignantly. "We've only been giving him leftovers. Mommy said it's silly to waste food."

"In addition to his regular meals?"

"But, Daddy, we can't let him *starve*—"

"He's in no danger of starving. No wonder he's gotten so voracious. You've accelerated his appetite as well as his growth. I told you not to do that. Well...it's over now. We should have done this a long time ago." Filltree picked up the net and brought it around slowly, approaching Rexy from his blind side, taking great care not to alarm the two-foot tyrant king. The thing was getting large enough to be dangerous.

Rexy hissed and bit at the net, but did not try to run. Tyrannosaurs did not have it in their behavior to run. They attacked. They ate. If they couldn't do one, they did the other. If they couldn't do either, they waited until they could do one or the other. The creatures had the single-mindedness of lawyers.

Working quickly, Filltree caught Rexy in the net and swung him up and over the glass fence of the terrarium. He lowered the dinosaur into the open carry cage, turned the net over in one swift movement to tumble the creature out, lifted it away, and kicked the lid shut. He latched it rapidly before Rexy could begin bumping and thumping at it with his head. Jill watched, wide-eyed and resentful. She had stopped crying, but she still wore her cranky-face.

"What are you going to do with him?" she demanded.

"Well, he's going to spend tonight in the service porch where it's warm. Tomorrow, I'm going to take him to…the dinosaur farm, where he'll be a lot happier." To the animal shelter, where they'll put him down…for a hefty fee.

"What dinosaur farm? I never heard of any dinosaur farm."

"Oh, it's brand new. It's in…Florida. It's for dinosaurs like Rexy who've gotten too big to live in Connecticut. I'll put him on an airplane and send him straight to Florida. And we can visit him next year when we go to Disney World, okay?"

"You're lying—" Jill accused, but there was an edge of uncertainty in her tone. "When are we going to Disney World?"

"When you learn to stop whining. Probably when you're forty or fifty." Filltree grunted as he lifted the carry cage from behind. He could feel its center of gravity shifting in his arms as Rexy paced unhappily within, hissing and spitting and complaining loudly about being confined. The little tyrant was not happy. Jill complained in unison. *Neither* of the little tyrants were happy.

Somehow Filltree got the heavy box up the stairs and into the service porch. "He'll be fine there till tomorrow, Jill." In an uncharacteristic act of concession, he said, "You can feed him all the leftovers you want tonight. The harm has already been done. And you can say goodbye to him tomorrow before you go to school, okay?"

Jill grumped. "You're not fair!" she accused. She stomped loudly out of the service porch and upstairs to her bedroom for a four-hour sulk, during which time she would gather her strength for the daughter of all tantrums. Filltree waited until after he heard the slam of her door, then exhaled loudly, making a horsey sound with his lips. Considering the amount of agita produced, he wondered if he'd locked up the right animal.

Dinner was the usual resentful tableau. The servitors wheeled in, laid food on the table, waited respectfully, wheeled back, then removed the plates again. His wife glared across the soup at him. His daughter pouted over the salad. Not a word was said during the fish course. Instead of meat, there was soy-burger in silence again. Filltree had decided not to speak at all if he could possibly avoid it. Joyce couldn't start chewing at him if he didn't give her an opportunity.

Idly, he wondered how much meat it would take to accelerate Rexy's growth to six feet tall. The idea of Rexy stripping the flesh from Joyce's bones and gulping it hungrily down gave him an odd thrill of pleasure.

"What are you smiling about?" Joyce demanded abruptly.

"I wasn't smiling—" he said, startled at having been caught daydreaming.

"Don't lie to me. I *saw* you!"

"I'm sorry, dear. It must have been a gas pain. You know how soy-burger disagrees with me."

He realized too late his mistake. Now that the conversational gauntlet had been flung, picked up and flung back, Joyce was free to expand the realm of the discussion into any area she chose.

She chose. "You're being very cruel and unfair, you know that," she accused. "Your daughter loves that animal. It's her *favorite*."

Filltree considered the obvious response: "That animal gets more hamburger than I do. I'm the breadwinner in this family. I'd like to be treated as well as Rexy." He decided against it; that way lay domestic violence and an expensive reconciliation trip to Jamaica. At the very least. Instead, he nodded and agreed with her. "You're right. It is cruel and unfair. And yes, I know how much Jill loves Rexy." He tasted the green beans. They were underdone. Joyce had readjusted the servitors again.

"Well, I don't see why we can't rebuild the terrarium."

"It isn't the terrarium," Filltree pointed out quietly. "It's Rexy. He's been accelerated. Nothing we do is going to contain him anymore." He resisted the temptation to remind her that he had warned her about this very possibility. "If he gets any bigger, he's going to start being a hazard. I don't think we should take the risk, do you?" He inclined his head meaningfully in Jill's direction.

Joyce looked thwarted. Jonathan had hit her with an argument she couldn't refute. She pretended to concede the point while she considered her next move. Perhaps it was just the shape of her new coiffure, but her expression seemed ominous and calculating. Filltree wondered why he'd ever wanted to marry her in the first place.

His wife patted the tinted hairs at the back of her neck and smiled gently. "Well, I don't know how you intend to make it up to your daughter…but I hope you have something appropriate figured out." Both she and Jill looked to him expectantly.

Filltree met their gaze directly. He returned her plastic smile with one of equal authenticity. "Gee, I can't think of anything to take Rexy's place."

Joyce tightened her lips ever so delicately. "Well, I can. And I'm sure Jill can too, can't you sweetheart…?" Joyce looked to Jill. Jill smiled. They both looked to Daddy again.

So. That was it. Filltree recognized the ploy. Retreat on one battlefield, only to gain on another. Jamaica appeared inescapable. He considered his options. Option. Dead end. "You've already made the booking, haven't you?" His artificial smile widened even more artificially.

"I see," his wife said curtly. "Is that what you think of me…?" He recognized the tone immediately. If he said anything at all—*anything*—she would escalate to tactical nukes within three sentences. The *worst* thing he could say would be, "Now, sweetheart—"

Instead, he opened his mouth and said, "We can't go, in any case. I have research to do in Denver." This time, he amazed even himself. Denver? Where had *that* idea come from? "I'll be gone for a month. Maybe two. At least. I'm sorry if this ruins your plans, dear. I would have told you sooner, but I was hoping I wouldn't have to go. Unfortunately…I just heard this afternoon that no one else is available for this job." He spread his hands wide in a gesture of helplessness.

Joyce's mouth tightened almost to invisibility—then reformed itself in a deliberate smile. "I see," she said, in a voice like sugared acid. She refused to lose her temper in front of Jill. It was a bad role model, she insisted. She had declared that eight years ago, and in the past five, Jonathan Filltree had amused himself endlessly by seeing how close to the edge he could push her before she toppled over into incoherence. Tonight—with Denver—he had scored a grand slam home run, knocking it all the way out of the park and bringing in all three runners on base. "We'll talk about this later," she said with finality, her way of admitting that she was outflanked and that she had no choice but to retreat and regroup her energies while she reconnoitered the terrain. She would be back. But for the moment, the conversation was temporarily suspended.

"I'll be up late," Filltree said genially. "I have a report to finish. And I have to pack tonight too." He took a healthy bite of soy-burger. It was suddenly delicious.

Joyce excused herself to escort Jill upstairs to get her ready for bed. "But, Mommy, don't I get dessert…" the child wailed.

"Not while your Daddy is acting like this—"

Jonathan Filltree spent the rest of the evening, working quietly, almost enjoying himself, anticipating what it would be like to have a little quiet in the house without the regular interruption of Rexy's intolerable predations. If only he could get rid of Jill and Joyce as easily.

Filltree wondered if he should sleep on the couch in his office tonight, but then decided that would be the same as admitting a) that there had been a battle, and b) he had lost. He would not concede Joyce one inch of territory. Before heading upstairs, he took a look in at Rexy.

The tyrannosaur was worrying at the left side wall of the carry cage, scratching at it with first one foot, then the other, trying to carve an opening for itself. It bumped its head ferociously against the side; already the thick polymoid surface was deformed and even a little cracked. Filltree squatted down to get a closer look at the box, running his hands over the strained material. He decided that the damage inflicted was not sufficient to be worrisome; the carry cage would hold together for one more day. And one more day was all he needed.

He headed upstairs to bed, smiling to himself. It was a small victory, but a victory nonetheless. The knowledge that he'd be paying for it for months to come didn't detract from the satisfaction he took in knowing that he'd finally held the line on something. Today, Rexy; tomorrow, the soy-burger.

He was awakened by screaming—unfamiliar and agonized. Something was crashing through the kitchen. He heard the clattering of utensils. Joyce was sitting up in bed beside him, screaming herself, and clawing at his arm. "Do something!" she cried.

"Stay here!" he demanded. "See to Jill!" Wearing only his silk boxers, and carrying a cracked hockey stick as his weapon, he went charging down the stairs. The screaming was getting worse.

A male voice was raging, "Goddammit! Get it off of me! Help! Help! Anyone!" This was followed by the sound of someone battering at something with something. High-pitched shrieks of reptilian rage punctuated the blows.

Filltree burst through the kitchen door to see a man rolling back and forth across the floor—a youngish-looking man, skinny and dirty, in bloody T-shirt and blue jeans. Rexy had his mouth firmly attached to the burglar's right arm. He hung on with ferocious determination, even as the intruder swung and battered the creature at the floor, the walls, the stove. Again and again. The screaming went on and on. Filltree didn't know whether to strike at the burglar or at the dinosaur. The man had been bitten severely on both legs, and across his stomach as well. A ragged strip of flesh hung open. His shirt was soaked with blood. Gobbets of red were flying everywhere; the kitchen was spattered like an explosion.

The man saw Filltree then. "Get your goddamn dinosaur off of me!" he demanded angrily, as if it were Filltree's fault that he had been attacked.

That decided Filltree. He began striking the man with the hockey stick, battering him ineffectively about the head and shoulders. That didn't work—he couldn't get in close enough. He grabbed a frying pan and whanged the hapless robber sideways across the forehead. The man grunted in surprise, then slumped to the floor with a groan, no longer able to defend himself against Rexy's predacious assault. The tyrant-lizard began feeding. He ripped off a long strip of flesh from the fallen robber's arm. The man tried to resist, he flailed weakly, but he had neither strength nor consciousness. The dinosaur was undeterred. Rexy fed unchecked.

Behind him, Joyce was screaming. Jill was shrieking, "Do something! Daddy, he's hurting Rexy!"

Filltree's humanity reasserted itself then. He had to stop the beast before it killed the hapless man; but he couldn't get to the net. It was still in the service porch—and he couldn't get past Rex. The creature hissed and spit at him. It lashed its tail angrily, as if daring Filltree to make the attempt. As if saying, "This kill is mine!"

Filltree held out the frying pan in front of him, swinging it back and forth like a shield. The small tyrant-king followed it with its baleful black eyes. Still roaring its defiance, it snapped and bit at the frying pan. Its teeth slid helplessly off the shining metal surface. Filltree whacked the creature hard. It blinked, stunned. He swung the frying pan again and, reflexively, the dinosaur stepped back; but as the utensil swept past, it stepped right back in, biting and snapping. Filltree recognized the behavior. The beast was acting as if it were in a fight with another predator over its kill.

Filltree swung harder and more directly, this time not to drive the creature back, but to actually hit it and hurt it badly. Rexy leapt backward, shrieking in fury. Filltree stepped in quickly, brandishing the frying pan, triumphantly driving the two-foot dinosaur back and back toward the service porch. As soon as Rexy was safely in the confines of the service porch, screaming in the middle of the broken remains of the carry cage, Filltree slammed the door shut and latched it—something went thump from the other side. The noise was punctuated with a series of angry cries. The door thumped a second time and then a third. Filltree waited, frying pan at the ready…

At last, Rexy's frantic screeching ebbed. Instead, there began a slow steady scratching at the bottom of the door.

When Filltree turned around again, two uniformed police officers were relievedly reholstering their pistols. He hadn't even heard them come in. "Is that your dinosaur, sir?"

Shaken, Filltree managed to nod.

"Y'know, there are laws against letting carnivores that size run free," said the older one.

"We'd have shot him if you hadn't been in the way," said the younger officer.

For a moment, Filltree felt a pang of regret. He looked at the fallen burglar. There was blood flowing freely all over the floor. The man had rolled over on his side, clutching his stomach, but he was motionless now, and very very pale. "Is he going to make it—?"

The older officer was bending to examine the robber. "It depends on the speed of the ambulance."

The younger cop took Filltree aside; she lowered her voice to a whisper. "You want to hope he doesn't make it. If he lives, he could file a very nasty lawsuit against you. We'll tell the driver to take his time getting to the E.R. …"

He looked at the woman in surprise. She nodded knowingly. "You don't need any more trouble. I think we can wrap this one up tonight." She glanced around the room. "It looks to me like the burglar tried to steal your dinosaur. But the cage didn't hold and the creature attacked him. Is that what happened?"

Filltree realized the woman was trying to do him a favor. He nodded in hasty agreement. "Yes, exactly."

"That's a mini-rex, right?" she asked, glancing meaningfully at the door.

"Uh-huh."

"Lousy pets. Great guard-animals. Do yourself a favor. If you're going to leave him running loose at night, get yourself a permit. It won't cost you too much, and it'll protect you against a lawsuit if anyone else tries something stupid."

"Oh, yes—I'll take care of that first thing in the morning, thank you."

"Good. Your wife and kid know to be careful? Those Rexys can't tell the difference between friend and foe, you know—"

"Oh, yes. They know to be *very* careful."

Later, after the police had left, after he had calmed down Joyce and Jill, after he had cleaned up the kitchen, after he had had a chance to think, Jonathan Filltree thoughtfully climbed the stairs again.

"I've made a decision," he said to his shaken wife and tearful daughter. They were huddled together in the master bedroom. "We're going to keep Rexy. If I'm going to be in Denver for two months, then you're going to need every protection possible."

"Do you really mean that, Daddy?"

Filltree nodded. "It just isn't fair for me to go away and leave you and Mommy undefended. I'm going to convert the service porch into a big dinosaur kennel, just for Rexy. Good and strong. And you can feed him all the leftovers you want."

"Really?"

"It's a reward," Filltree explained, "because Rexy did such a good job of protecting us tonight. We should give him lots and lots of hamburger too, because that's his favorite. But you have to promise me something, Jill—"

"I will."

"You must *never* open the kennel door without Mommy's permission, do you understand?"

"I won't," Jill promised insincerely.

Turning back to Joyce, Filltree added, "I promise, I'll finish up my work in Denver as quickly as possible. But if they need me to stay longer, will that be okay with you?"

Joyce shook her head. "I want you to get that thing out of the house tonight."

"No, dear—" Filltree insisted. "Rexy's a member of our family now. He's earned his place at the table." He climbed into bed next to his wife and patted her gently on the arm, all the time thinking about the high price of meat and Rexy's insatiable appetite.

THE SEMINAR
FROM HELL

After a moment, the sad-looking woman approached the registration table. Her husband followed with visible resignation. "Is this the... seminar?" the woman asked with obvious embarrassment.

The attractive young hostess behind the table smiled warmly at the both of them. Her nametag identified her as Tia. "Yes, you're in the right place. This is the Nine Circles Corporation. Welcome to our Introduction Seminar." She slid two beige cards across the table to them, and two pencils as well. "Please fill out a guest card."

The woman hesitated. "Nobody's going to call us, are they? We don't want to be pressured."

"We don't pressure people," Tia said. "And yes, we do make one follow-up call to find out if you enjoyed the evening or have any additional questions or concerns that didn't get answered."

"We just don't want our name on some list...."

Tia's smile was warm and sincere. "You're our guests. We like to know who you are."

The woman sighed and picked up the pencil. She filled out the card slowly. Tia pushed the other card at the husband. Reluctantly, he followed his wife's lead. Both of them looked sorry and ashamed, as if by being here, they were admitting all the failures of their lives. They finished filling in their names and addresses and passed the cards back.

Tia glanced at the tan guest cards, and quickly filled out two name-tags. "Here you are, Maggie," she twinkled. Robot-like, Maggie peeled off the backing and stuck the nametag to her coat. "And here's yours, George. Thank you for being here."

"Do I have to wear a nametag?" George glowered at the invasion.

"Yes, I'm afraid so. The Seminar Leader likes to know who he's talking to."

"Who's leading the seminar?" George asked suspiciously.

"His name is Steven Keyes, and you'll find that he's absolutely the *best*. If you have any questions at all, just ask any of the assistants who are wearing gold nametags like mine." Tia indicated the badge over her heart. "I'm sure you'll have a great time tonight. The promise of this evening is that abundance is your divine right."

"Divine?"

"That's right," Tia said. "The Nine Circles Corporation is committed to success—*everyone's*."

"Yeah?" George grunted skeptically. "What's the catch?"

Tia's bright smile deflected George's remark as if it hadn't even been spoken. "All your questions will be answered in the seminar, I'm sure." She gestured toward the waiting door. "I hope you enjoy yourselves."

Maggie plucked at her husband's sleeve in a gesture that said more than "Let's go in." It also implied, "Please don't make a scene." In the language of husbands and wives, the shorthand was unmistakable. George allowed himself to be pulled away and the two of them headed nervously toward the meeting room. Tia turned her attention to the next group of people waiting to sign in.

Inside, the rows of chairs were filling quickly. Maggie kept her gaze low. As curious as she was, she didn't really want anyone else to see her here. If she didn't look around, she believed, then no one else would have the right to look back at her. Nevertheless, after a moment, her curiosity won out and she began taking sly peeks at the other people in the room.

All around them, snappily dressed assistants stood at strategic intervals, smiling and eager to serve. All of the assistants looked healthy and fresh. One vigorous-looking fellow glided up and asked them to please fill up the seats toward the front. After a moment's hesitation, George and Maggie complied without argument, but they moved deeper into the room with obvious reluctance. Sitting too close to the front would make it harder to sneak out later if they got uncomfortable with what they were hearing.

"Well, they're certainly slick," George muttered resentfully as he took his seat. He folded his arms across his chest; his signal that he had brought his body here, but not his willingness.

When almost all of the chairs were filled, someone in the back began applauding. Soon, everyone was clapping excitedly. Then, as the applause reached its peak, the seminar leader came up the center aisle from the back of the room and leapt happily onto the stage—he almost bounced, he was so light on his feet. Although his hair was a graceful mane of white, he seemed ageless. He wore a light tan suit that glittered like gold. Maggie thought he looked like a movie star; George thought he looked like a Hollywood phony.

"Hello!" he called broadly. "Good evening! How are you? This isn't television—you can say hello back!" He looked out over the room, as if recognizing everyone there and acknowledging the applause of all of them. "Thank you, thank you," he said, smiling and waving at all the guests and assistants.

"Thank you all for that very warm welcome," he began when the applause finally died down. "My name is Steven Keyes, and I'm the seminar leader from Hell." He paused to acknowledge the laughter. Some of it was very nervous. "I want to thank you all for being here tonight. I know there are a lot of other places you could be. Not many people want to go to Hell. And certainly not on a school night." More laughter, this time a lot less nervous. It was all right to laugh here.

"In fact," he added, "Most people don't even want to *know* about Hell, so I have to acknowledge your courage just for coming into the room. "That's right." He nodded, sharing his understanding with them.

Maggie settled herself in her seat comfortably. Whatever else he might be, Mr. Keyes was certainly charming. She had no intention of signing up for anything, but at least she could enjoy listening to what he had to say. She glanced over at George. His expression remained a resolute frown.

"Listen—" Steven Keyes held up a hand, grinning out at the crowd. "You've got to recognize the difficulty of my job here. Most people come in here, they've already got their minds made up. Hell isn't a nice place. And those of us who speak for it aren't to be trusted. Yes? Admit it—how many of you came in here tonight just a little bit afraid for your immortal souls? Hold up your hands high. That's right. Hold 'em high so everybody can see. Look around...."

Despite themselves, George and Maggie slowly raised their hands. They glanced quickly around at the rest of the room and saw that most of the other people wearing guest-tags were also holding their hands up in the air.

"You see?' said Steven Keyes. "You're not alone. Okay, you can put your hands down now." His smile disappeared and he became deadly serious for a moment. "I want you to notice something here. Despite being afraid, just like you, all of these people still showed up. *You* showed up. *Why?* Because...despite what you've heard, despite what you think, despite what you might be afraid of, you are still *curious* enough that there might be something here—something that just might be worth your taking the time to find out *more* about it." Steven Keyes glanced around the room, shifting his gaze from person to person, and for a moment, Maggie felt he was looking straight into her heart. She glanced quickly at George, but if he had felt anything, he didn't show it.

"You want to acknowledge yourselves for that," Keyes said with almost painful directness. "Yes, you do. Because you're not letting someone else's opinion keep you from finding out for yourselves what Nine Circles really has to offer. You didn't let someone else tell you—"

Abruptly, he interrupted himself to make an additional point, gesturing with certainty and confidence. "Listen, I know how difficult it was to get here. A few years ago, I was sitting out there where you are now, wondering what kind of a con game or racket this was. And there were people in my life too who were telling me not to come, just like there are probably people in your life too who have told you that this is the wrong thing to do. They've probably said something like, 'Be careful! Don't put yourself at risk!' Am I right?" He glanced around the room. Several of the guests were nodding in agreement. He laughed; the sound was infectious. "I *am* right, aren't I?

"Well, do you want to know something?" Steven Keyes asked rhetorically. "Your friends were right. There *is* a risk here. But you've already mastered it. Just by being here, you're taking the chance that you might discover a way to be more effective and successful in your life than you have ever dreamed of before.

"You see, success—*real success*—is all about taking risks. You know that. You don't win anything by being comfortable. Comfort is a dead-end. It's a trap. Nine Circles is not about being comfortable. It's about being effective, successful, and powerful—and *enjoying* yourself every moment of it. And that means taking the biggest risk of all, *letting go of the past so you can grab hold of the future.*

"You had to take that risk to be here tonight. You had to risk being wrong in what you believed about us. You had to risk making the people around you wrong. You probably annoyed the hell out of your husbands, your wives, your family members, when you told them you were coming. Yes? I'll bet many of you have put some of your best friendships at risk just by being here. Yes? Yes?"

Maggie nodded to herself. She glanced over at George. He still had his arms folded across his chest, but he was listening.

"And you know what *else* you had to risk?" Keyes continued. "You had to risk your arrogance. That's right—*your arrogance*. Each of us, we're kind of arrogant in our lives. Yes, we are. We think we've got it all pretty well figured out. We know how to survive—and we do. We survive very well—so well in fact, that for a lot of us, mere survival looks a lot like success. Sometimes we get so good at it that we think survival *is* success.

"But, listen to me—it's all that attention on survival that keeps getting *in the way* of success. To succeed, you have to be willing to *not* know. You have to be willing to give up what you do know to find out what you don't know. And that means you have to give up your arrogance—and that's what you've done by being here. And I thank you for that. You've acknowledged that you can't afford the arrogance of not knowing something, the knowing of which might very well transform the quality *of the rest of your life.*"

Maggie's forehead creased in puzzlement. She wasn't sure she understood exactly what he was saying. Some of it sounded like pyscho-babble, techno-jargon to her; but she was sure that Steven Keyes understood it, and if she just listened hard enough, perhaps she would get it too. Beside her, George was also frowning again.

"Look," said Steven Keyes, as if he was responding directly to her thoughts. "This isn't weird. It isn't mysterious. It's really very simple. What we're offering is the possibility that there's another whole way to *be*. It's the chance to have everything you've ever wanted, right here, right now. You shouldn't have to wait for your rewards. You're entitled to them *now*. You've earned them. It's just that simple."

He held up a hand as if to stop himself. "I'm not stupid. You're not stupid. We *all* know that you can't get something for nothing. That's the way the universe works. The Nine Circles Corporation is offering a service here—and you want to know what it's going to cost you.

"I know what the *other side* has said about us. So do you. The other side says that we're trying to trick you out of your immortal soul...." He looked around the room expectantly, smiling and nodding. "Yes?" he asked. "Isn't that what they say?" He held up his hands again, spreading them wide and open. "But did you ever stop to ask yourself what is the other side *trying* to do? *What do they want?*"

Keyes waited a moment, letting his audience consider the answer to that question. He looked around the room, studying their faces, watching to see if his words had had the desired effect. They had. Some of the faces looked angry, others looked amused, still others were worried at the implication of the thought.

Maggie had never considered this thought before. It troubled her. She slipped her hand sideways, into George's. He let her put her hand in his, but she could tell he was too preoccupied with his own thoughts to acknowledge the gesture.

"Listen," Steven Keyes was saying. "You don't need me to tell you. You've heard it all your life what *they want* from you—not what they're going to do for you, but what you have to do for them. They want you to forego the pleasures and rewards of this world. In return, they promise you the *unspecified* pleasures and rewards of the next world. They want you to live a life of deprivation and sacrifice, they want you to live in guilt and shame for all of your days, confessing and repenting your sins, begging their forgiveness, so you can attain worthiness—*but in exchange for what?* Just what are the rewards of the next world? Have you ever noticed that they never tell you!"

Keyes sounded angry, as if raging at a colossal betrayal. His anger resonated throughout the room. Maggie glanced around nervously. Other people looked equally unhappy with this news. She didn't know how she felt about it. She felt torn and confused.

"I'll tell you what they want," said Keyes. "They want the same thing we do. They *want* your immortal soul! That's right—*they* want your souls too." He stepped forward to the edge of the podium, leaning out toward his audience. "And they don't even have the honesty to offer you something in exchange for it. *They* just keep saying, 'Trust me!' Well, you're big boys and girls. You know what 'trust me' means in the real world. You've been there. Would you trust anyone who isn't willing to sign a contract? Would you buy a car that way? Or a house? Why would you trust your immortal soul to someone who says, 'Trust me?' We offer you signed contracts. Do they? No—but they'll give you all the *faith* you want. Try spending *that* at the supermarket."

Keyes was clearly warming to his subject now. He'd let his temper flash, just enough to be interesting. Now, he allowed his good-natured geniality to surface again. He unbuttoned his gold jacket; he hitched his thumbs into his waist band, and he stepped down off the podium and began pacing up and down the aisles like a high school math teacher drilling his students. He looked directly into people's eyes and spoke to them like old friends. Maggie put her fist to her chin and chewed worriedly on a nail. She didn't like this part.

"Let me tell you something," Steven Keyes said. "This is a business. I get paid for doing these talks. But even if I didn't get paid, I'd still do it, because I love the chance to work with people like you, people who care about themselves and their families and their futures. I have a family too. And a future. And I came to an event like this six years ago, just as worried as you about the direction my life was going. I'd lost my faith in the product offered by the *other side*. I'd tried it their way for nearly forty years and it didn't work. That's right. I'm forty-five years old. And no, I don't look it, do I? I've been invigorated. And you can be invigorated too. Listen—I was desperate. My life was a mess.

"Oh, my life looked ideal to those who didn't know. My wife and I had kids and dogs and two cars and a swimming pool and a house in the suburbs—but we weren't *happy*. We weren't having fun. The joy had leached out of our marriage and our lives. And one morning, I found myself standing in front of the mirror, thinking about work, thinking about family, thinking about bills and problems and all the little things that kept going wrong, thinking about gray hairs and gray days stretching out in front of me until I dropped dead either of a coronary or cirrhosis of the liver, thinking and thinking and holding my razor and wondering whether I should shave or slash my wrists—and that's when I knew I needed to *do something*.

"What I did was this—" He pointed to the floor where he stood. "I accepted an invitation to come to one of these seminars. And I came here just as skeptical and worried and fearful as each and every one of you probably is right now. I had just as many questions and concerns. And yes, I was just as apprehensive as you are now about being conned one more time—especially this time, when the stakes look to be so high. So I know what you want to hear, what you *need* to hear. Because I've been there myself.

"Let me start at the beginning. This used to be a protected market, this little rock we're living on. Six thousand years ago, nobody believed that human beings represented much of a commodity, certainly not a worthwhile market. Most of the services offered here in the far past were mom-and-pop operations, strictly local, strictly small-time. It wasn't until the Yahweh Corporation was granted a license for development that real growth became possible.

"Now, look. I'm not going to say bad things about them—that's not good business, in any case. And the fact is, they did a great job in elevating this market to a whole new standard of productivity in a very short time—only six thousand years. Look around. We're not shepherds anymore. We're a major industrial world. And that's the point. This market is now large enough and successful enough that it can support free competition. You deserve it. You've earned it. You have a right to a fair choice. That's what this is.

"They've had their monopoly long enough. They've made their money back, a long time ago. Now it's time to open up this arena. Over a thousand years ago, the Nine Circles Corporation began petitioning to have this market expanded. We've had to work very hard to prove ourselves—we've had to run a lot of pilot projects, but we've finally been granted full license to compete here. And that's put a real scare into the Yahweh people. So they're saying a lot of bad things about us, hoping to keep you so scared about who we are and what we represent that you won't even consider our services.

"Listen—they've had sole custody of the market for nearly six thousand years. Do you know what's happened to them? They've forgotten how to play on a level field. They've gotten complacent, lazy, and arrogant...and worst of all, they aren't delivering the services they're promising. And that's not fair to you, because you have no other supplier—*until now*."

Keyes still paced around the room. He stopped and looked directly at George and Maggie, startling them both in their chairs. "I know what you're thinking. No—not because I read minds. I don't. I know it because

I've been there myself. You're asking yourself, the same way I did, six years ago, 'What is this wonderful product anyway?'" George shifted uncomfortably in his seat. Maggie felt flattered at the personal attention.

"Well, I'm going to tell you." Keyes said. "The product is something so intangible that when I tell you, you won't really hear me. You won't hear what I'm saying—you'll hear what you want to hear, or what you're afraid to hear, or what you think you hear. You won't hear what I'm saying because it won't get past what you're already hearing. So you'll shrug it off. You'll dismiss it. You'll disregard it as trivial. Maybe, you'll even be annoyed that I've spent so much time talking about something so simple. Or maybe you'll say, 'Oh, hell, Steven, I already knew that.' Yes, you will. This isn't the first time I've delivered this talk—and the truth is, you aren't unique. That's the bad news. The good news is that our product works. It works better than you imagine. It works better than you *can* imagine. And best of all, it works *a hell of a lot better than theirs!*" Keyes grinned broadly, nodding and looking around the room, once again meeting the eyes of all of the guests. "So, here's what you've got to do," he said. "You've got to listen to me as if the quality your life depended on it—because it does!" He continued looking and nodding, waiting until the room was absolutely silent and every eye was fixed directly on him.

"What is our product?" he asked again, rhetorically. "Very simple. What we're selling here is *a whole other way to be.* Let me say that again. We are offering you an opportunity to change your way of *being.* You will stop being the way you have been, the way that doesn't produce the results you want, and take on instead a *new* way to be, a way that *does* produce the results you want. It's that simple.

"You know—" Keyes interrupted himself again, dropping back into his friendly conversational tone. "There's a very interesting definition of what it is to be crazy. Do you know what being crazy is? Albert Einstein defined it. It's doing the same thing over and over and over, again and again, each time expecting a different result. Well, that's what the other side is telling you to do. That's the product that the other side is offering you. Have faith. Trust. Pray. Sacrifice. Be patient. And you'll get what you want. Someday. Not now, though. No matter what you ask for, that's their answer. Someday. And they expect you to be stupid enough to believe that, to take that on faith—to have that same answer produce different results this time, when it hasn't produced any results before! That's crazy!

"Let's face it! Their way of being doesn't work!" Keyes accused, suddenly and angrily stabbing the air with his finger. "If it did, you wouldn't be here—not even out of curiosity!" He began moving about the room again, weaving his way up one aisle and down the next, pausing only to touch people on the shoulder or pat them reassuringly. "Look, I know it's tough out there. You know what everybody says, you've heard it, you've probably said it yourself: *'Life is hard. Then you die. Then they throw dirt in your face. Then the worms eat you. Be grateful it happens in that order.'* He laughed along with the rest of the room. "Yeah, we laugh. It's funny. If we didn't laugh, we'd have to cry. Like that's something to be grateful for—right?

"If their way is so wonderful, how come so many of us are out of work? How come so many of us are going to bed hungry? How come so many of us have no place to live? If their way is so wonderful, how come there's so much evil in the world? Have you ever asked yourself that? Sure you have. Have you ever come up with a satisfactory answer?

"I know what *their* answer is—they blame us. They say it's *our* fault. That's their answer for everything—to blame the opposition. Notice that they *never* take responsibility for their own way of being!

Steven Keyes stepped back up to the dais at the front of the room and allowed his raw anger to show again. "The truth is, we've all been conned, dominated, manipulated, cheated, beaten up, beaten down, and used until we're all used up. And after a while, we think that's normal. Well, it isn't. It isn't normal. It isn't natural. *It isn't right!*"

Keyes was nearly shouting now. "And all it takes to change it is you being willing to make the commitment to change it. You've got to say, 'I'm sick and tired of being sick and tired.' You've got to say, 'I mad as hell and I won't take it any more.' You've got to say, 'I won't have it!' You've got to say, 'I deserve a fair share! I deserve the best!'

"That's right. You do. And I'm going to tell you how to have it." He stepped over to the podium and lifted up a single sheet of paper with a crisp black writing on it, easily readable. "See this? This is our contract. We're willing to put it all in writing. It's a legally binding document. When you read it, you'll see that it compels us to produce specific measurable results, a tangible change in your situation for the better, resulting in your personal satisfaction. If you're not satisfied—and you're the *only* arbiter of whether or not you are satisfied— but if you're not satisfied, then the contract is null and void.

"If we do satisfy you, then all we ask you to do is share this work with your friends. Ten friends. Twenty. As many as you want. Don't worry—once you're successful, you're going to have a lot of friends, and they're all going to want to know how you got so successful and effective and happy. Bring them to one of our seminars. We have seminars every week. We'll give them the same opportunity as you.

"Listen, you can have your lawyer look at this contract. You can have a hundred lawyers look at it. I promise you, it'll stand up in court. It's legal and binding and it compels the Nine Circles Corporation to produce results. When was the last time you signed a contract with this kind of a guarantee? Think about it. Not in this lifetime, right? *Right?*"

Around the room, people were nodding. Even George grunted a reluctant assent. Maggie glanced at him in surprise.

"And what do we get in return? What's the catch?" Steven Keyes asked the question with a sudden quiet solemnity that startled the room back into intense silence. "*They* tell you that we want your immortal soul. That's what *they* tell you. But *they* want your soul too. So the real catch is that we're offering you a choice and they're telling you that you have *no choice.* How does that make you feel? Angry? Yes? That's how it made me feel too. Well, I'm telling you that you *do* have a choice.

"You see, the *real* question is not who wants your soul—but *what* are they going to do with it once they get it?"

"They don't tell you that, do they? Just what are they going to do with your immortal soul that's so wonderful? I mean, there's this whole wonderful mythology about heaven and how great it's supposed to be, but just ask one of its representatives what heaven is really like and listen to what he or she says. Do you believe those stories? I don't. Is that the kind of place *you* want to spend eternity? I don't.

"Now, let's be honest with each other. Let's get past the mythology and the fairy tales and the glittering generalities and duck-billed platitudes. Let's talk specifics.

"There's no such place as Hell. Not like they tell you. There's no fires. No devils. No damnation. No eternal torment. I promise you that. I've been there. I've seen it. It's actually a very nice place. By the way, there's no such place as Heaven either. That's just as big a lie.

"Now, you've probably been told by your friends not to believe me; that I'll probably lie about Hell just to trick you. But I want you to stop a moment and think. Really *think* about the concept of Hell that they keep insisting is the truth. It's a pretty sick idea, isn't it? Can you imagine a just and compassionate deity plunging his children forever into the fires of eternal damnation just for making a mistake? Would you treat *your* children that way? Of course not. No *sane* person would. So why would a god, who's supposed to be omniscient and omnipresent, all-knowing and all-wise and all-loving, behave like a psychotic thug? That doesn't make sense, does it?

"You want to know what's really going on—both Heaven *and* Hell? I'll tell you."

Steven Keyes stepped down from the dais and began walking through the room again. Once more he touched the people he spoke to. He held their hands, he patted their shoulders, he held is hand against one woman's cheek. He dropped to his knees beside George and Maggie. "Listen to me. The whole point of this is to experience the adventure of yourself to the *fullest*—to live passionately! Your job is to look and listen and smell and touch and feel! Your job is to be alive and do all the things that people do when they are fully and completely alive! Roar with anger, weep with fear, laugh with joy, cry with sorrow—build, fight, love, plan, enjoy! The whole point of being alive is to experience yourself as a piece of the universe, to learn something about what it means to be a human being...*so you can bring that lesson back to the godhead.*

"The Yahweh company—they want you to believe what they tell you to believe, because they want to redesign the godhead in their own image. We don't agree with that. The Nine Circles Corporation wants you to have the most successful and powerful life you can. We want you to love the life you're living. We want you to be effective and masterful and satisfied. We want you to learn as much about the way the universe works as possible. And then...when it's time to fulfill the contract, we want you to bring that knowledge and joy into the godhead that we represent. We want to make you powerful, so you can bring your power back to us when you've mastered it. We want to make you wise, so you can bring that wisdom back to us when you've gained it. We want to have you satisfied, so you can add the wealth of your satisfaction to the larger satisfactions of our company. We want to make you strong, so you can incorporate your strengths into our body of thought. We want to make you stronger and wiser and happier, so that you can help make the Nine Circles Corporation stronger and wiser and happier. That's the deal. It's that simple."

Steven Keyes went back to the front of the room. "Now, here's what it's going to take," he said. He held up the contract again. "In a minute, we're going to have an opportunity for you to sign one of our contracts. There are tables at the back of the room. There are tables at the sides of the room. Our assistants—the good-looking young men and women in the gold nametags—are there to answer your questions and help you fill in your contract. All you have to do is list what you want out of life and then sign your name at the bottom. Be specific. Demand miracles. You'll get them. I promise you.

"But, remember, you're going to have to put yourself at risk," Keyes said directly. "And risk is scary. Especially *this* risk. Let me tell you something about risk. No matter what you do, it's all the *same* risk. You're stepping off into the unknown. It *always* feels like you're stepping off the top of a building. But *not* taking the risk is to stay stuck where you are. Is that where you want to be? So let me tell you what happens after you step off the top of the building. Most people just scream—all the way down. But, here's what happens when you step off the top of *our* building—*you get to look in all the windows!*

"That's right. You're still going to end up at the bottom—a big red splotch on the sidewalk—but the difference is that you're going to have much more fun on the way down." Keyes stopped himself. He held up his hand. He became serious again. "Listen, you took one big step just being here tonight. You took the risk that maybe—just *maybe*—there might be something to this. This is the opportunity to take the other half of that risk...to make the commitment to be the person you've always wanted to be. But what you have to give up is the person you think you are now.

"Let me say that again. It's important. You have to give up who you think you are so that you can discover who you're going to become. You're going to have to give up the past to grab hold of the future.

"Now, I know where you are with this. You're probably in one of three places. Some of you in this room are ready to jump. And when we take the break, you'll go right back to the table and sign up. Some of you may never be ready, and you're not going to sign up. And that's okay too. Thank you for being here. Thanks for coming to find out what we're up to. And last, some of you are poised on the edge, not quite ready to go, not quite ready to say no, because you think you want to think about it a little bit longer. If you're in that place, I just want to say one thing to you. I want to ask you one question. How much jogging do you get done thinking about jogging? You have to seize the moment—or the moment passes without you.

"So, here's how to know if you should sign up. Ask yourself what you most want out of life. Ask yourself if you're getting it. Ask yourself if you can expect to get it if you keep on doing what you're doing now. If the answer is no, then you had better start thinking about doing something else, hadn't you? That's right.

"So here's the something else to do. Go to one of the tables. Pick up a copy of our contract. Read it. Read it carefully. Even if you're not planning to sign up tonight, read one of our contracts, so you can satisfy yourself as to our integrity. If there's anything you don't understand—*anything* at all—then have one of our assistants explain it to you. Don't worry. Our assistants won't let you sign anything until you fully understand *exactly* what it is you're signing. And then...when you're ready, *sign it*. Yes, an ordinary ball-point pen is sufficient." Steven Keyes flashed one last genial grin. "All right, thank you again for being here. Let's do it now—all those who want to go to Hell with me, come to the tables and sign your contracts." He waited until the last of the applause died down and then he stepped down off the dais and headed up the aisle to the tables at the back of the room.

A buzz of excited noise began. People stood up, some of them stretching, some of them heading straight for the tables. Maggie turned and looked to George. "I want to do it," she said quietly.

George's hands had fallen to his lap. They were old and rough and battered-looking. He seemed to be studying them, but Maggie knew better. He had withdrawn into thoughts. She'd seen him do this before. Whenever he felt pressured, he disappeared inside himself. He simply wouldn't respond.

"George," she said insistently, refusing to be ignored this time. "I want to be happy. I want you to be happy. I'm going to sign up." She reached over and put her hand on his shoulder. "I want you to sign up with me."

Slowly, he lifted his gaze. He turned heavily to look at her. His eyes were rheumy and shaded with years of unspoken sadness. When he spoke his voice was barely audible. "I can't," he said. "I—I'm afraid."

She was astonished by his honesty. "There's nothing to be afraid of," she tried to reassure him. "These people won't hurt us—"

"No," he shook his head. "I'm not afraid of dying. I've been dying all my life...." For a moment, Maggie thought he was through speaking, but then he managed to croak out the last of the thought. "I'm afraid... of living."

Maggie let the words hang in the air between them while she studied his face. "Fine," she said, finally. "I'll do it without you then." After a moment more of waiting, she got up and headed for the table at the back of the room.

George watched her go, his eyes filling up with years of shame and failure.

...AND EIGHT RABID PIGS

It's not that I hate Christmas, I don't. I just don't want to be around when it's celebrated.

I suppose I should explain. It really goes back a few years. You probably don't remember Steven Dhor, do you? No, I didn't think so. Nobody does any more.

Okay, do you remember *Ominous* magazine? It only lasted for ten issues, but it had stories by some of the best fantasy and horror writers in the business. Steven Dhor made his first sale to *Ominous*. And three other sales too. He was one of the best. Really. His mind was always running. You could tell. There was a fire in his heart; you could see it blazing in his eyes. He loved storytelling. He loved working an audience. There was that special interaction that occurred. You could see him prowling the halls of the hotel looking for the right parties, the right people to talk to.

The hotel? Oh, conventions. Horror and fantasy conventions. Dhor liked to go to the cons. He said the whole of writing was finding the right place to sit. You put down roots and the story grows. Dhor was a great talker. People loved to listen to him. He loved the whole process of inter-acting with a disparate group of minds and watching what would happen when they started playing.

He'd start by throwing out a seed. Sometimes I don't think he even realized he'd done it. Things just happened in conversation, and then someone would respond, and then the next thing you knew Dhor would seize the moment. He'd hold up his hands and say, "Wait, wait—" And then, when the room fell silent, he'd start building something. With the right people in the group, feeding him curious notions and bits of phraseology, Steven Dhor would turn into a whole other kind of person—like a golden boy, he glowed in the light. You had to be there. He was mesmerizing.

You know how a crow will steal shiny objects for its nest? Well, that was Dhor. He'd swoop down from the sky and pluck the most glittering notions out of a conversation, and then a week or a month later, you'd see them again, woven into the fabric of whatever story he had just finished.

He read his stories aloud at conventions. He had this very gentle, deceptively high-pitched voice. He had such a melodious way of talking, he lulled you with it. You never expected such a sweet voice say such horrible things. Women were fascinated by him. So were men. But none of them could ever touch him. And they all tried. Oh, he did his share of sleeping around, with both sexes—I don't think he was a bisexual; I think he was a thrill-sexual—but he never got involved with anyone for longer than a weekend.

He liked people, but…for him, I think the real love affair was with ideas—always ideas. I guess individuals never really interested him. He was much more fascinated by the things that happened in the dark corners of the universe. Like horrible deaths, strange murders, disappearances—and revenge. He *loved* revenge.

Not because he was a vengeful person. He wasn't. See, that was the thing. In person, he was always so sweet and kind and gentle that you couldn't believe he really meant any of it. It was like he was just playing with you, you refused to take him serious. But he believed that storytellers were the Research and Development division for the human race. He said writers were the world's only real specialists in revenge. And it was our duty to invent the most interesting, elegant, and sophisticated revenges that we could. I heard him do this talk several times. He'd ask people for the best revenges they could think of. Most of the time, I think he was disappointed. He was always looking for the best revenge he could. Like ground glass in the vaseline. That was one of his favorites. He used it in one of his stories, *The Bloodied Lance*. You didn't see that one either, did you? No, you'd have remembered it if you had. It was nasty.

Anyway...eventually, I began to think that maybe Steven wasn't as sweet and gentle as we wanted to believe. It was his Christmas story. Most people have forgotten it by now, but it caused a real uproar at the time. *Ominous* published it in their special Christmas issue, and some of the advertisers were so upset that they cancelled their contracts and I think that's one of the reasons the magazine folded. But the story as it was published was the edited-down version. The real story was much longer than that. And much more graphic.

I'll tell you how it started. There was a convention, I don't remember which one, they're all alike, and a bunch of us were sitting around in the bar, Bread Bryan was there, all tall and spindly like a frontier town undertaker. Railroad Martin was there—in the official Railroad Martin uniform, T-shirt, jeans, and pot belly. George Finger was there; I think he was between wives and illnesses. And maybe a couple of others. Anyway, we were talking about something Goodman Hallmouth had said—of course, you've heard of Goodman. Everybody has.

Anyway, Goodman had shown up to collect the *Ghastly* Award for most horrifying display of manners at a banquet, or something like that, and during one of his panels, he'd made the statement that for most people Santa Claus is more real than God; at least, Santa Claus gives you a tangible reward. And then from there, he'd expanded his thesis that the whole concept of Santa Claus is nothing more than the large-scale brainwashing of children into a Christian ethic. If you're good, you get a reward, a present; if you're bad, you get a lump of coal. If you're good all your life, you get a reward, you get to go to heaven; if you're bad, you go to hell.

Santa Claus is not only most people's first experience of God, Hallmouth had said, it's now their *only* experience of God, because the religious significance had been taken out of Christmas by the courts. The only non-denominational displays allowed any more were pictures of Santa Claus, reindeer, Christmas trees, snowmen, and the like.

Hallmouth had been in fine form that day. He'd gone on at length about how this country was economically addicted to Christmas. We'd turned it into a capitalist feeding frenzy—so much so that some retailers depended on Christmas for fifty percent of their annual business. Hallmouth wanted us to "Just Say No to Christmas." Or at least—for God's sake—remember whose birthday it was and celebrate it appropriately, by doing things to feed the poor and heal the sick. And then he'd taken up a collection for his charity. You didn't dare not put something in the jar.

I had missed the Hallmouth performance this year. I'd gotten tired of the performance of angry young rabble-rouser, about the time Hallmouth had turned fifty, and knowing that after he finished rousing the rabble, he was going to demand money for the performance, I'd decided to skip the performance.

So, there we were in the bar, and we were talking about this and that and the other thing, and abruptly, Steven Dhor said, "Y'know, if Hallmouth is right—that Santa Claus is an expression of God, then there has to be a demonic clause in that charter too. A Satan Claus. There has to be a balance in the universe."

"Satan Claus," echoed Bread Bryan. "Mm. He must be the fellow who visited my house last year. He didn't give me anything I wanted. And I could have used the coal too. It gets *cold* in Wyoming."

"No. Satan Claus doesn't work that way," said Dhor. "He doesn't give things. He takes them away. The suicide rate goes up around Christmastime. That's no accident. That's Satan Claus. He comes and takes your soul straight to hell."

"Yep," said Railroad Martin. "And he drives a black sleigh and he lands in your basement."

"The sleigh is drawn by eight rabid pigs—razorbacks," said Dhor, "and they have burning red eyes, which glow like smoldering embers— they *are* embers, carved right out of the floor of hell. Late at night, as you're lying all alone in your cold, cold bed, you can hear them snuffling and snorting in the ground beneath your house. Their hooves are polished black ebony, and they carve up the ground like knives."

Dhor was creating a legend while we sat and listened enraptured. He held up his hands as if outlining the screen on which he was about to paint the rest of his picture. We fell silent, and he said, "Satan Claus travels underground through dark rumbling passages filled with rats and ghouls. He carries a long black whip, and he stands in the front of the sleigh, whipping the pigs until the blood flows from their backs. Their screams are the despairing sounds of the eternally tormented."

"And he's dressed all in black," suggested Bread Bryan. "Black leather. With silver buckles and studs and rivets."

"Right," agreed Martin. "Black leather. But the leather is made from the skins of reindeer."

"Whales," said Finger. "Baby whales."

Dhor shook his head. "The leather is made from the skins of those whose souls he's taken. He strips it off their bodies before he lets them die. The skins are dyed black with the sins of the owners, and trimmed with red-dyed rat fur. Satan Claus has long gray hair, all shaggy and dirty and matted; and he has a long gray beard, equally dirty. There are crawly things living in his hair and beard. And his skin is leprous and covered with pustules and running sores. His features are deformed and misshapen. His nose is a bulbous monstrosity, swollen and purple. His lips are black and his breath smells like the grave. His fingernails are black with filth, but they're as sharp as diamonds. He can claw up through the floor to yank you down into his demonic realm."

"Wow," said Bread Bryan. "I'm moving up to the second floor."

We all shuddered at Dhor's vivid description. It was a little too heavy for the spirit of the conversation. A couple of us tried to make jokes, but they fell embarrassingly flat.

Finally, George Finger laughed and said, "I think you've made him out to be too threatening, Steve. For most of us, Satan Claus just takes our presents away and leaves changeling presents instead."

"Ahh," said Railroad. "That explains why I never get anything I want."

"How can you say that? You get T-shirts every year," said Bread.

"Yes, but I always want a tuxedo."

After the laughter died down, George said, "The changeling presents are made by the satanic elves, of course."

"Right," said Dhor. He picked up on it immediately. "All year long, the satanic elves work in their secret laboratories underneath the south pole, creating the most horrendous ungifts they can think of. Satan Claus whips them unmercifully with a cat o' nine tails; he screams at them and beats them and torments them endlessly. The ones who don't work hard enough, he tosses into the pit of eternal fire. The rest of them work like little demons—of course they do, that's what they are—to manufacture all manner of curses and spells and hexes. All the bad luck that you get every year—it comes straight from hell, a gift from Satan Claus himself." Dhor laughed wickedly in that sweet gentle laugh of his, and everybody laughed with him.

But he was on a roll. He'd caught fire with this idea and was beginning to build on it now. "The terrible black sleigh isn't a sleigh as much as it's a hearse. And it's filled with bulging sacks filled with bad luck of all kinds. Illnesses, miscarriages, strokes, cancers, viruses, flu germs, birth defects, curses of all kinds. Little things like broken bones and upset stomachs. Big things like impotence, frigidity, sterility. Parkinson's disease, cerebral palsy, multiple sclerosis, encephalitis, everything that stops you from enjoying life."

"I think you're onto something," said Railroad. "I catch the flu right after Christmas, every year. I haven't been to a New Year's party in four years. At least now I have someone to blame."

Dhor nodded and explained, "Satan Claus knows if you've been bad or good—if you've been bad in any way, he comes and takes a little more joy out of your life, makes it harder for you to want to be good. Just as Santa is your first contact with God, Satan Claus is your first experience of evil. Satan Claus is the devil's revenge on Christmas. He's the turd in the punch bowl. He's the tantrum at the party. He's the birthday-spoiler. I think we're telling our children only half the story. It's not enough to tell them that Santa will be good to them. We have to let them know who's planning to be bad to them."

For a while, there was silence, as we all sat around and let the disturbing quality of Dhor's vision sink into our souls. Every so often someone would shudder as he thought of some new twist, some piece of embroidery.

But it was my speculation that ended the conversation. I said, "Y'know, this might be a dangerous line of thought, Steve. Remember the theory that the more believers a god has, the more powerful he becomes? Well, I mean, it's a joke right now, but aren't you summoning a new god into existence this way?"

"Yes, Virginia," he said to me, absolutely deadpan, "There *is* a Satan Clause in the holy contract. But I don't think you need to worry. Our belief in him is insufficient. And unnecessary. We can't create Satan Claus—because he already exists. He came into being when Santa Claus was created. A thing automatically creates its opposite, just by its very existence. You know that. The stronger Santa Claus gets, the stronger Satan Claus must become in opposition."

See, Steven had been raised in a very religious household. His grandmother had taught him that for every act of good, there has to be a corresponding evil. Therefore, if you have heaven, you have to have hell. If you have a God, you have to have a devil. If there are angels, then there have to be demons. Cherubs and imps. Saints and damned. Nine circles of hell? Nine circles of heaven. And I guess he believed it. For the rest of the weekend, he went around poking people and saying, "Better be careful! Satan Claus is watching." And then he'd cackle fiendishly. I guess he thought he was being funny, but for some reason, his remarks left a very bad smell in my head. At the time I wasn't sure why.

I forgot about Satan Claus for a few weeks. I was involved in another one of those abortive television projects—it's like doing drugs; you think you can walk away from them, but you can't. Someone offers you a needle and you run to stick it in your arm. And then they jerk you around for another six weeks or six months, and then cut it off anyway—and one morning you wake up and find you're unemployed again. The money's spent, and you've wasted another big chunk of your time and your energy and your enthusiasm on something that will never be broadcast or ever see print. And your credential has gotten that much poorer because you have nothing to show for your effort except another dead baby. You get too many of those dead babies on your resume and the phone stops ringing altogether.

Yeah, I guess that was the summer of my discontent. That was when I finally quit banging my head against the walls of the glass cage and tried to rediscover my love of storytelling. One afternoon, I stopped by Kicking The Hobbit—the all science-fiction bookstore that used to be in Santa Monica—and there was Steven Dhor, doing an autograph party and a reading of a new story. He waved to me as I came in, but kept on reading to a large crowd of entranced listeners: "*...the children believed that they could hear the hooves of the huge black pigs scraping through the darkness. They could hear the snuffling and snorting of their hot breaths. The pigs were foaming at the mouth, grunting and bumping up against each other as they pulled the heavy sled through the black tunnels under the earth. The steel runners of the huge carriage sliced across the stones, striking sparks and ringing with a knife-edged note that was neither a shriek nor a scream, but something of both.*

"*And the driver—his breath steaming in the terrible cold—shouted their names as he whipped them, 'On, damn you, on! You children of war! On Pustule and Canker and Sickness and Gore! On Monster and Seizure and Bastard and Whore. Drive on through the darkness! Break through and roar!*" His voice rose softly as he read these harrowing passages to his enraptured audience. It took me a moment to realize, but the meter of the passage gave it away. He had turned his speculations about Satan Claus into another one of his vivid and terrifying nightmare visions.

I hung back away from the group, but listened in spite of myself. A dark chill was growing at the bottom of my spine. If Goodman Hallmouth's passionate diatribe against the obscene capitalization of Christmas carried any merit, then this act of Dhor's was an even more outrageous act—a sacrilegious perversion. By the very act of saying the name aloud in public, Dhor was not only giving his power to Satan Claus, he was daring the beast to visit him on Christmas Eve.

"*...And in the morning,*" Dhor concluded, "*—there were many deep, knife-like scars in the soft dark earth beneath their bedroom windows. The ground was churned and broken and there were black sooty smudges on the glass...But of their father, there was not a sign. And by this, the children knew that Satan Claus was indeed real. And they never ever laughed again, as long as they lived.*" (Selections from "The Blight Before Christmas" by Steven Dhor, are reprinted here with permission of the literary estate of Steven Dhor.)

The small crowd applauded enthusiastically, and then they crowded in close for autographs. I gave Dhor a noncommittal wave, and left the store. I was very disturbed, but I couldn't say why.

Look, I'm not one of those who believe that "there are some things man was not meant to know." That's the world's shortest story. On the contrary, I think that if you can ask the question, then you have the right to search for the answer. But I also think there's a corresponding responsibility. Our words create realities for people. They believe in what we write. At some point, we have to stop and ask ourselves—what are we creating? What effect are we having on the people who read our stories? Are we harming them or helping them?

I know—some people say, "Oh, heck, we're just competing for their beer money. All we're doing is giving them a little entertainment." But I don't think that's enough. Entertainment is such a shallow goal. Isn't it possible that entertainment is just the carrier wave on which the real information is being carried? Isn't it possible that the way we entertain people has a profound effect on the way they live their lives? If we continue to portray revenge as an appropriate response to a situation, aren't we also condoning and creating that behavior?

I'd been walking around with that question in my head for a long time. I'd done my share of entertainment. I'd looked out into the sea of vacuous faces and found myself wondering if this was truly important, truly worth the effort. Now, listening to Steven Dhor read his story of gleeful viciousness and theological perversion, I realized that it was wrong to put such imagery into an unsuspecting reader's head. By the time I got home that evening, I think I had resolved never to write another word of horror again.

Dhor called me a week later, about something else, but in the course of the conversation, he asked me what I thought of his Satan Claus story. I told him, I didn't think it was funny. I thought it went beyond the bounds of good taste. I thought it was despicable. He wasn't pleased with my remarks. Maybe it was a mistake for me to be so candid, but he asked me, so I answered. He told me I was arguing against the art and that was why I would always be a second rate writer. Then he hung up. His words stung me badly, but I'd made him angry enough to say what he really thought. I knew that we'd probably both apologize the next time we saw each other, but our relationship would never again be comfortable; it would always contain that core of suspicion and distrust. Already, Satan Claus was beginning to exert his first tendrils of power.

I saw Dhor several more times that year. And everywhere I ran into him, he was reading that damned story aloud again: *"Christmas lay across the land like a blight, and once again, the children huddled in their beds and feared the tread of heavy bootsteps in the dark...."* He'd look up from the pages, look across the room at me with that terrible impish twinkle and then turn back to his reading with renewed vigor. I began to suspect Dhor was doing it deliberately, because he knew it annoyed me. *"...Millie and little Bob shivered in their nightshirts as Daddy pulled them onto his lap. He smelled of smoke and coal and too much whiskey. His face was blue and scratchy with the stubble of his beard and his heavy flannel shirt scratched their cheeks uncomfortably. 'Why are you trembling?' he asked. 'There's nothing to be afraid of. I'm just going to tell you about the Christmas spirit. His name is Satan Claus, and he drives a big black sled shaped like a hearse. It's pulled by eight big black pigs with smoldering red eyes. Satan Claus stands in the front of the carriage and rides like the whirlwind, lashing at the boars with a stinging whip. He beats them until the blood pours from their backs and they scream like the souls of the damned—'"* Finally, I refused to stay in the same room with him. In the weeks that followed, he read it at the fund-raiser/taping for Mike Hodel's literacy project. He read it at the Pasadena Library's Horror/Fantasy Festival. He read it at the

Thanksgiving weekend Lost-Con. He read it on Hour 25, and he had tapes made for sale to anyone who wanted one.

"'Satan Claus comes in the middle of the night—he scratches at your window, and leaves sooty marks on the glass. He comes through the wall like smoke and stands at the foot of your bed with eyes like hot coals. He stands there and watches you. His hair is long and gray and scraggly. His beard has terrible little creepy things living in it. You can see them crawling around. Sometimes, he catches one of the bugs that lives in his beard and he eats it alive. If you wake up on Christmas Eve, he'll be standing there waiting for you. If you scream, he'll grab you and put you in his hearse. He'll carry you straight away to Hell. If you get taken to Hell before you die, you'll never get out. You'll never be redeemed by baby Jesus…'"

And then *Ominous* came out and everybody was reading it. At least, it seemed that way.

"Little Bob began to weep and Millie reached out to him, trying to comfort him; but Daddy gripped her arm firmly and held her at arm's length. 'Now, Millie—don't you help him. Bobby has to learn how to be a man. Big boys don't cry, Bobby. If you do, for sure Satan Claus will come and get you. He won't even put you in his hearse. He'll just eat you alive. He'll pluck you out of your bed and crunch your bones in his teeth. He has teeth as sharp as razors and jaws as powerful as an axe. He'll bite your arms off and your legs—and even your little peepee. And then he'll bite your head off! So you mustn't cry. Do you understand me!' Daddy shook Bobby as hard as he could, so hard that Bobby's head bounced back and forth on his shoulders and Bobby couldn't help himself; he bawled as loud as he could."

People were calling me on the phone and asking me if I'd seen the story and what did I think. Wasn't it the scariest story I'd ever heard? "Are you going to recommend it for a Nebula Award?" they asked.

At first, I tried to explain why I felt it was an evil story—but nobody was listening. Sometimes, I had the eeriest feeling that I was talking to converts to a new religion. They were having too much fun playing with the legend of Satan Claus, adding to it, building it—giving their power of belief to the horror crawling through the ground below us.

"'Listen! Maybe you can hear him even now? Feel the ground rumble? No, that's not a train. That's Father Darkness—Satan Claus. Yes, he's always there. Do you hear his horn? Do you hear the ugly snuffling of the eight rabid pigs? He's coming closer. Maybe this year he's coming for you. This year, you'd

better stay asleep all night long. Maybe this year, I won't be able to stop him from getting you!'"

Then some right-wing religious zealot down in Orange County saw the story; his teenage son had borrowed a copy of the magazine from a friend; so of course the censorship issue came bubbling right up to the surface like a three-day corpse in a swamp.

Dhor took full advantage of the situation. He ended up doing a public reading on the front steps of the Los Angeles Central Library. The L.A. Times printed his picture and a long article about this controversial new young fantasy writer who was challenging the outmoded literary conventions of our times. Goodman Hallmouth showed up, of course—he'd get up off his death bed for a media event—and made his usual impassioned statement on how Dhor was exposing the hypocrisy of Christmas in America. Give me a break.

"The children trembled in their cold, cold beds, afraid to close their eyes, afraid to fall asleep. They knew that Father Darkness would soon be there, standing at the foot of their beds and watching them fiercely to see if they were truly sleeping or just pretending."

It all came to a head at Art and Lydia's Christmas Eve party. They always invited the whole community, whoever was in town. You not only got to see all your friends, but all your enemies as well. Lydia must have spent a week cooking. She had huge platters piled with steaming turkey, ham, roast beef, lasagna, mashed potatoes, sweet potatoes, tomatoes in basil and dill, corn on the cob, pickled cabbage, four kinds of salad, vegetable casseroles, quiche and devilled eggs. She had plates of cookies and chocolates everywhere; the bathtub was filled with ice and bottles of imported beer and cans of soda. Art brought in champagne and wine and imported mineral water for Goodman Hallmouth.

And then they invited the seven-year locusts.

All the writers, both serious and not-so, showed up, some of them wearing buttons that said, "Turn down a free meal, get thrown out of the Guild." Uh-oh. Artists too, but they generally had better table manners. One year, two of them got trampled in the rush to the buffet. After that, Lydia started weeding out her guest list.

I didn't find out until after I had already gotten in the door and removed my coat, but this year, the unofficial theme of the party was "Satan Claus is coming to town." The tree was draped in black crepe and instead of an angel on top, there was a large black bat.

"Little Bob still whimpered softly. He wiped his nose on his sleeve. Finally, Millie got out of her bed and crept softly across the floor and slipped into bed next to little Bob. She put her arms around him and held him close and began whispering as quietly as she could. 'He can't hurt us if we're good. So we'll just be as good as we can. Okay. We'll pray to baby Jesus and ask him to watch out for us, okay?' Little Bob nodded and sniffed, and Millie began to pray for the both of them....."

I got there late.

Steven Dhor was holding court in the living room, sitting on the floor in the middle of a rapt group of wanna-bes and never-wases, embellishing the legend of Satan Claus. By now, I'd already heard the rumor that he was planning to do a collection of Satan Claus stories, or perhaps even a novel telling the whole story of Satan Claus from beginning to end. Just as St. Nicholas had been born out of good deeds, so had Satan Claus been forged from the evil that stalked the earth on the night before Jesus' birth.

According to legend—legend according to Dhor—the devil was powerless to stop the birth of baby Jesus, but that didn't stop him from raising hell in his own way. On the eve of the very first Christmas, the devil turned loose all his imps upon the world and told them to steal out among the towns and villages of humankind and spread chaos and dismay among all the world's children. Leave no innocent being unharmed. It was out of this beginning that the legend of Satan Claus came forth.

"The children slept fitfully. They tossed and turned and made terrible little sounds of fear. Their dreams were filled with darkness and threats. They held onto each other all night long. They were awakened by a rumbling deep within the earth, the whole house rolled uneasily—"

Dhor had placed himself so he could see each new arrival come in the front door. He grinned up at me, as if to say, "See? You were wrong. Everybody loves it." I frowned back at him and shook my head. He didn't understand. He probably never would. I turned away and went in search of the hosts. I'd brought them a bottle of Chateau Marmoset or something like that.

"They came awake together, Millie and little Bob. They came awake with a gasp—they were too frightened to move.

"Something was tapping softly on the bedroom window. It scraped slowly at the glass. But they were both too afraid too look."

Lydia was dressed in a black witch's costume, she even wore a tall pointed hat. She was in the kitchen stirring a huge cauldron of hot mulled wine and cackling like the opening scene in Macbeth, "Double, double toil and trouble, fire burn and cauldron bubble—" and having a wonderful time of it. She saw the look on my face and stopped. "What's the matter? Did your dog die?"

I shook my head. "I'm sorry, I just don't think Satan Claus is very funny."

"Aww, come on—" she laughed. "Aren't you just a little tired of elves and snowmen every year?"

"No, actually, I'm not. To tell the truth, I'd rather celebrate Jesus' birthday instead of the evil that preceded his coming."

She patted my arm. "You are too good for your own good."

I handed her the wine. "Here. I don't think I'm going to stay very long—"

"A huge dark shape loomed like a wall at the foot of their bed. It stood there, blocking the dim light of the hallway. They could hear its uneven heavy breath sounding like the inhalations of a terrible beast. They could smell the reek of death and decay. Millie put her hand across little Bob's mouth to keep him from crying.

"'Oh, please don't hurt us,' she cried. She couldn't help herself. 'Please—'"

I circulated once through the party, shaking hands, wishing people well, trying not to show my unease. I mumbled apologies. No, I wasn't staying. I'd just stopped by to say hello and drop off a little gift for the host and hostess. Good to see you again. Yes, you too. I'll call you next year. Please give my love to your mom. No, I really can't stay, thanks.

"But, you're going to miss it—Steve is going to read a new Satan Claus story at midnight!"

"I'll have to catch it another time." A weak smile and a weaker handshake. I practically bolted for the door.

"And then—a horrible thing happened. A second shape appeared behind the first, bigger and darker. Its crimson eyes blazed with unholy rage. A cold wind swept through the room. A low groaning noise, somewhere between a moan and an earthquake resounded through the house like a scream. Black against a darker black, the first shape turned and saw what stood behind it. It began to shrivel and shrink. The greater darkness enveloped the lesser, pulled it close, and—did something horrible. In the gloom, the children could not

clearly see; but they heard ever terrible crunch and gurgle. They heard the choking gasps and felt the floor shudder with the weight.

"Millie screamed then, so did little Bob. They closed their eyes and screamed as hard as they could. They screamed for their very lives. They screamed and screamed and kept on screaming—"

I heard later that Steven Dhor got very drunk and had to be driven home about two in the morning. Bread Bryan and Railroad Martin took him home and poured him into bed. He was unconscious at the time.

The next morning, he was gone.

I stopped by his place on Christmas morning, I'd wanted to apologize; but he didn't answer. I walked around the back and banged on the back door too. Still no answer. I peered in his bedroom window, and his bed was disheveled and empty. I assumed he'd gotten up early and left, perhaps to spend Christmas with a friend. I didn't know him well enough to guess who he might have gone to see.

Later, I heard that he was missing. But by then, it didn't surprise me. I'd already begun to suspect.

His landlady assumed he'd skipped town to avoid paying his rent. Goodman Hallmouth said he thought Steven had gone home to visit his family in Florida and would probably return shortly. Bread Bryan said that Steve had mentioned taking a sabbatical, a cross-country hitchhiking trip. Railroad Martin filed a missing person report, but after a few routine inquiries, the police gave up the investigation. George Finger suggested that Satan Claus had probably taken him, but under the circumstances, it was considered a rather tasteless joke and wasn't widely repeated.

But…I saw the evidence. There were sooty smudges on his bedroom window, and the ground beneath the window was all torn up and churned, as if by the milling of many heavy-hoofed creatures.

ADDENDUM

Even at this late date, the power of the delusion remains undiminished.

The patient continues to believe in the existence of an actual supernatural being called Satan Claus. It is his belief that the act of creating and repeating the legend of Satan Claus called such a being into existence, and that the individual known as Steven Dhor was devoured on Christmas Eve by a physical manifestation of this demonic entity.

While he remains entirely lucid and able to converse rationally about almost every other subject, the patient is unable to recall even the smallest details of his previous life. He continues to insist that the writer Steven Dhor is dead and that he (the patient) is only a colleague of much lesser fame ability. Curiously, he does not question why he is here.

If one accepts that the Satan Claus delusion has devoured the creative center of the patient's consciousness, then the rest of the patient's identity can only avoid the same fate by pretending to be someone else. Only by hiding within himself can he avoid attracting the further attentions of the demon brooding within his soul.

Patient remains extremely dangerous. Medication levels should be continually monitored.

(signed) Olin Whitaker, Ph.D.

CHESTER

After the accident, Annie was all I had left. She had a limp, she had a scar down the right side of her face that her hair couldn't quite cover, and sometimes she had a look in her eyes that worried me—not quite frightened, resigned.

Six year old girls were supposed to be happy spring butterflies, bouncing from one bright-colored moment to the next. But the giggles of the season were silent. Annie sat alone in her room, holding her doll, the one with the smashed face, and stared at the wall. Not even out the window.

The doctors said she needed time, that's all. She'd been through a lot, and she still missed her mother—but she'll come back to life eventually. When she's ready.

But nobody's ever ready for anything. I knew that. I wasn't ready to be a widower at thirty-three.

I sat down next to Annie and put my arm around her shoulders. She didn't resist, but neither did she relax. She let me pull her close, but she was still a little zombie. I leaned over and sniffed her hair, kissed the top of her head, and whispered into her ear, "Have I told you today how much I love you?" She didn't respond.

Out of frustration, as much as anything else, I scooped her up and held her on my lap, hugged her close. "You're my favorite kid in the whole wide world and that's never going to change." I stroked her hair. "Listen to me, sweetheart. I know it hurts. I miss her too. But maybe we can help each other. You know how I come in here and talk to you about what I'm feeling? Well, maybe sometimes if you wanted to talk to me, maybe you could do that and maybe that would help a little bit. What do you think?"

Not even a nod. I knew she heard me, but when she got like this, she seemed unreachable. Words like traumatized and catatonic and withdrawn all flashed through my head, but I hated those words—because the way that people used them, they stopped being descriptions, they became explanations. They turned into life-sentences.

"Okay, sweetheart, I'm not going to force you. When you're ready, you come see me, okay? Just say 'okay.' Okay?"

"Okay," she whispered. And that was enough. Not quite a breakthrough, but certainly the possibility of one.

"I'm going to go make dinner now. Let's have something special. Just for us. What would you like? I'll make your favorite."

"Pancakes."

"Pancakes for dinner? Okay, that sounds fun. And bacon too? Will you come help?"

In this case, help meant sitting silently on her chair while I flipped pancakes on the griddle. When I put the plate in front of her, she made no move to eat. "Didn't I do them right?"

"Daddy, I'm scared."

"Of my pancakes?"

"No. Don't be *silly*."

"Okay." At least she was talking. "What *are* you scared of?"

"Going to sleep."

"Going to sleep?"

"I'm afraid…I won't wake up."

My first instinct was to say, "That's silly. Everybody wakes up." But I stopped myself in time, because that wasn't true. We both knew that. So instead, I just nodded knowingly, "Yeah, that is scary." I had a dozen questions I wanted to ask, but I didn't want to push too hard. It was more important that she knew it was safe to talk.

I reached over and began cutting her pancakes for her. She could do it, but before the accident she had always asked me. She used to say "I like the way you do it, Daddy." But today, she pushed my hands away and said, "I'll do it myself."

"Okay." I sat down opposite her and busied myself with my own plate. I wasn't very hungry, but I went through the motions anyway, waiting for her to go on.

"There's this thing in my dream," she said very matter-of-factly.

"What kind of thing?"

"I don't know. It's too dark and fuzzy to see. It's all flickery. It comes from *underneath*."

"Underneath?"

"Uh-uh. *Underneath*."

"Underneath what?"

"Underneath *everything*."

"Okay. What does it do?"

"Nothing."

"Nothing?" Very carefully, not wanting to put her off, I said, "I don't know, Annie. That doesn't sound very scary to me."

"Well, it is."

"Why?"

"Because it's *there*." She pushed a piece of pancake around on her plate, mopping up syrup. She still hadn't eaten a bite. "It's even there in the daytime. Only I can't see it, because it's always behind me."

"Now, *that* sounds scary."

"It is."

"Mmm," I said. "We're definitely going to have to do something about this."

"You can't."

"I can't?"

"No."

"Why not?"

"Because it's from *underneath*."

"I see. That is serious. Tell me, who's bigger? You or it?"

She didn't answer.

"I'll bet I'm bigger...."

Still no reply.

"Well, certainly the two of us together are big enough."

This wasn't going anywhere. I'd have to try something else. How do you fight magical thinking? *With stronger magic.*

"I know what'll work."

She looked up at me. "What?"

"A dream catcher."

"What's a dream catcher?"

"Just what it sounds like. Take a bite of that pancake and I'll tell you more."

She did and I did. I didn't remember everything, so I made up what I didn't know. "A dream catcher is like a net for your dreams. You hang it over your bed and it catches all your bad dreams. Like a spaghetti strainer. And when it's full, you throw it out and make a new one."

Annie looked skeptical.

"It's an old Indian trick. I learned it from an old Indian. We'll make a dream catcher as soon as you finish dinner. We'll need some yarn and some feathers and maybe some sequins too. We'll look in Mommy's sewing box—" Oops. For a moment, she was almost interested, but as soon as I said *Mommy*, Annie shut down again. If only I hadn't opened my big mouth. If only.

If only I hadn't tried to make the light—

I got up and went to the sink. I started scrubbing the griddle in fast ferocious movements, furious at myself for having a big mouth, for being stupid, for everything.

"That's okay, Daddy. We can still do it. Mommy won't mind."

I nodded curtly. Maybe Annie wasn't the only one who needed strong magic.

Annie picked out her favorite colors of yarn, and I found some dowels in the garage, leftover from my kite-building period. We tied three of the dowels together to make a triangle, then strung a clumsy webwork of braided yarn and plastic beads across the center. We pulled bright-colored feathers out of Mommy's Halloween boa, it was always shedding anyway, and tied them in rainbow blossoms to each corner. We hung more feathers and beads from the bottom. Then we said some magic words over it and hung it on the wall over Annie's bed. "There. That'll catch all your bad dreams. Or my name isn't Mortimer Chuzzlefinger."

"Da-addy!" I hadn't heard that pronunciation in a while, with all the extra syllables. I hadn't realized how much I'd missed it.

"Oh, I forgot. My name *isn't* Mortimer Chuzzlefinger. But don't worry about it. This will still catch all your bad dreams. Snout's Honor. Now go brush your teeth and put on your nightie."

Annie went without argument. She didn't bounce, she limped. She had turned into a serious little soul. I missed my little girl, the one who giggled. I wondered if I'd ever hear her laugh again. I tucked her into bed and hugged her tightly. She accepted it, she even hugged back, but there was still something missing.

The difference between human beings and coyotes is that when the Acme Rocket-Launcher blows up in the coyote's face, he doesn't lose heart. He just goes back to the Acme catalog and orders something else. Human beings never recover from that first awful explosion. We might not walk around with our hair sticking out in charred frizzles and a scorched look of stunned amazement, but we never really regain our trust in a safe and orderly universe either. Once suspicious, we remain suspicious. That's what murders childhood innocence.

I looked in on Annie several times that night. She appeared to be sleeping soundly. The dream catcher was on the wall over her headboard where we'd carefully hung it. When she was little, I used to sit and watch her sleep, amazed that any little human being could be so beautiful, even more amazed that I could be so totally committed to protecting her from harm. I'd always thought of myself as self-involved to the point of selfishness, but having Annie in my life showed me otherwise. All I could think about was her smile, the trusting way she slipped her hand into mine, the giggles and the laughter. Everything else was ... just stuff. I finally went to bed, hopeful that maybe the dream catcher was a way to start again.

But early the next morning, even before the sun was up, she came to me crying. "Daddy, the dream catcher didn't work—"

I followed her back to her room, where she pointed at the wall. Our carefully constructed webwork had been shredded. The dowels were broken and the netting we'd strung had been pulled apart. For a moment, I had the distinct impression that something had fought its way out. I started to say, "Why did you break it—?" then stopped myself. This wasn't the time for accusations. I scooped her up instead, hugged her, stroked her hair, and whispered, "Wow. That was some bad dream. We're going to need a bigger dream catcher." She just held on tight and wouldn't look.

Later, after she was dressed, after she had gone outside to sit under the tree to talk with her stuffed penguin, I took the shredded construction off the wall and examined it. The feathers we'd tied to the corners were all chewed, but not soggy-chewed like a child might do—ragged-chewed as if by the teeth of rats. The dowels too had the same tiny teeth marks. The yarn we'd tied and strung to make a dream-net had been stretched and pulled apart. And for a moment, I wondered if this might be something more than just a child's bad dreams. I even pulled her bed away from the wall and went looking for holes in the baseboard. Nothing. Nothing at all.

I tossed the shredded dream catcher into the trash, where Annie wouldn't see it, and wondered if I should make another one. But why would Annie rip it apart? Some deeper, darker thing we hadn't gotten to yet? All I could do was guess.

After a while, I went out to the garage. We had three old tennis rackets that we'd bought at a yard sale for five dollars. I had some metal rods and some nylon fishing line, an old bicycle wheel, and even some piano wire. I could make an industrial strength dream catcher, one she couldn't destroy. Maybe I could show her that Daddy was still bigger and stronger than the worst bad dreams she could imagine. That might work.

With the garage door open, I could keep an eye on her while I worked. I started with the three tennis rackets. I used the piano wire to tie them together, with their heads at the center and the handles sticking out at angles. I sprayed the whole affair with shiny black enamel. After they dried, I attached this construction to the bicycle wheel. Now it needed some decoration.

I found what was left of an old kite, a nine-foot long strip of silver mylar that rippled in the sun; I cut it into ribbons, twisted the ribbons into twirls and wound it around the rim and the spokes of the bicycle wheel. I burrowed into the Christmas decorations and found a box of tinsel and another box of silvery snowflake ornaments. I stapled the tinsel to the handles of the tennis rackets, and attached the snowflakes to the nylon webbing at the sweet spot. When I was done, the whole thing was a pretty ghastly affair—but enormously sturdy; you could carry a bowling ball on it. It was a very serious-looking dream catcher.

When I called Annie to the garage to see the new dream catcher, she stared at it with an appraiser's eye. Finally, she said, "Okay." But it wasn't a signal of affirmation, it was an "okay" of resignation. Yesterday, she had been hopeful, willing to believe. After last night, she was neither.

All right, I had to think about this. Building the second dream catcher had been useful. It was something to do with my hands, something to distract me while my subconscious chewed over the real problem—Annie's belief that there was something underneath that wanted to get to her. I remembered the chapters about "magical thinking." Annie needed to believe in something stronger. We all did. That was the essential part of being human. So after dinner, we hung up the dream catcher and lit a pink candle and waved feather dusters at it and said some magical words—"By the power of Great Ghu, the God of the Ceiling, let this dream catcher be a barrier to all and everything that wishes harm to this household and all who live here." —but Annie's dispirited "okay" reduced the whole thing to a silly performance. If she didn't believe, it wouldn't work. She was at that age where children start to give up belief. So who knew?

"Daddy?"

"Yes, sweetheart?"

"Will you sleep with me tonight? Mommy always slept with me when I had bad dreams."

I hesitated—remembering everything Dear Abby always said about parents sleeping with children—but this was Annie and this was serious medicine, so I said, "Of course, I will."

I tucked her in carefully, then lay down next to her on top of the covers. She snuggled up next to me, pressing her back against my side. She was asleep almost immediately. That was a relief, neither one of us had been sleeping all that well. Not since the accident. The endless cycling of memory had become a chronic pummeling. There was no peace. The slightest noise or irritation and I'd be up. The one person I most needed to talk to was the person who wasn't here. Maybe that's what Annie was feeling. But for just this little moment, maybe we could almost pretend that everything was going to be all right. Except I knew better.

The limp, the scar—when Annie was a teenager, these would be almost impenetrable barriers between her and everybody else. These things would set her apart from the world of normal girls. Girls used gossip and manipulation for bullying—little games when they were little, horrendous games when they grew bigger. Sometimes, in the way they interacted, you could see them training to be future harpies, honing the pernicious skills of ripping out the hearts of the innocent. Annie was already self-conscious about her wounds; her teen years would be hell. I'd asked about cosmetic surgery, physical therapy, orthopedic repair, but the doctors said there wasn't a lot they could do now, maybe later. But later might be too late. Her spirit was crippled too.

Eventually, I fell into an uneasy sleep, a swirl of disturbing dreams. Urgent dreams. I had to hide. I had to find a safe place, the safest. I hurried downstairs, down an escalator, down and down—at the bottom,

I rushed around a corner, around a corner, ducked under the angle of the rolling stairs, down again, through a narrow hallway and down the cramped emergency stairs, into the cluttered basement, where I ducked behind some boxes—I found a tiny opening, a vent; no, not even that, just a narrow nook underneath the floorboards, I crawled sideways around an impossible angle, down into a deeper space, dark and bottomless, I climbed down the metal ladder, down and down, always downward, until I found the hatch into the pipes below the city—I padded through the dank underbelly of the world, sloshing through tubes illuminated by phantom iridescence, climbing into narrower and narrower pipes, until I found another ladder down, this one leading to ancient stone tunnels, maybe catacombs, I couldn't tell, except after a while, the walls were pulsing, lined with throbbing purple veins and bulbous growths, and farther down, cracks appeared in the walls, glowing red as embers, it was warm here, too warm, uncomfortably hot, molten lava seeping up through the floor, the edges of the rocky crust were limned with flame, I had to jump across the bubbling pits, bottomless chasms too, had I come so far that I would never find my way back? I knew this place. There was something here. Behind me. I turned around and—

Woke up with a startled grunt. My heart pounding.

I fumbled around for my flashlight, the big heavy one filled with a half-dozen D-cells. Held overhand, it could be used as a club. If necessary. I'd put it on the nightstand next to Annie's bed so she could look to see there were no monsters in the dark. I clicked it on myself. Yes, there were no monsters. I was actually relieved.

Padded off to the bathroom, fever dreams still resonant. Checked the thermostat. Opened the front door and sniffed the night. Thought about going to my own bed. Thought about a lot of things. Three O'clock in the morning thoughts. All the way down to the bottom one—why does the universe even exist? Why is there something instead of nothing?

I went to the kitchen and poured myself the last of the coffee, still sitting cold in the carafe; gave it a short ride in the microwave, then returned to Annie's room. I stood in the doorway, sipping half-heartedly at the bitter brew until it was cold and tasteless. I didn't want to get back into her bed. It was uncomfortable. But I didn't want to leave her alone either.

We had a big overstuffed chair in the den. I'd fallen asleep in it more than once, usually during some made-for-TV movie on the Lifetime channel. I pushed the chair into Annie's room, grabbed a pillow and a comforter, and made myself as comfortable as I could. I moved as quietly as I could through the darkness. I wasn't planning on staying up all night, watching, but if anything made a sound, I'd be right here. Just before settling in, I flicked on the flashlight, one last time, just to check, I don't know what made me do it—

—stopped. And stared. Above Annie's bed. My carefully constructed industrial-strength dream catcher had been chewed to bits, as if something with metal teeth had gnawed its way out. I lifted it off the hook on the wall, astonished and shaking my head and for the first time, honestly worried. Even a little scared.

Carried it into the kitchen and laid it on the counter. The fluorescent lights flickered on, momentarily dazzling me. What the bloody hell—? The bicycle spokes were pulled every which way, the rim of the wheel was bent; the nylon webbing of the tennis rackets was unstrung, with bent and broken strands pointing out at odd angles. It looked as if someone or something had deliberately picked it apart.

All right, there had to be a rational explanation. Maybe it was the tension of the wires, maybe I'd strung the whole thing so tight it had unraveled in the middle of the night. Except I hadn't heard a sound. My sleep had been so uncertain these past few weeks, even the slightest rustle was enough to bring me bolt upright in bed. I couldn't imagine this thing *twanging* apart above my head without my hearing something. Unless I'd been so tired, so exhausted, so lost in sleep, so down in the dream, could the sound of this thing pulling itself apart have triggered my dreams of descent—? *Underneath?*

No. I wasn't ready to go there yet. I'd read articles about "unexplainable" phenomena that occurred at the nexii of standing waves—electrical, radio, sonic, whatever. Maybe this was like the guy who could hear the six O'clock news on his fillings? Yes, he had voices in his head, but it was only the local Ted Baxter. I tried to remember what I'd read about counter-measures. Put a large bowl of water next to an open window. Hang tinfoil strips. Rearrange the furniture. Install a ground wire. Check your cables. It all sounded like more dream catcher stuff. Just another belief system.

I wasn't going to figure it out tonight. I went back to Annie's room and plopped down next to her again. She snuggled into my arm and two blinks later, sunlight was streaming in through the window, illuminating the dust motes like bars of blue silver. I glanced over, saw she was sleeping peacefully, so I eased myself out of bed and went into the kitchen to start breakfast.

Eventually, Annie wandered in, still rubbing her eyes. "How'd you sleep, sweetheart?"

"Okay, I guess."

"No bad dreams?"

"Uh-uh." And then she said, perceptively. "You had the bad dream for me, didn't you?"

"Yeah, I guess I did."

"Was it as bad as I said?"

I nodded. "Yeah, I can see why you were scared."

She glanced at the broken dream catcher. "That didn't work, did it?"

"I guess not." I started flipping pancakes. "We'll have to figure out something else."

We spent the day running errands, dropping things off, picking things up, maintaining all the separate machineries of suburbia. Annie didn't fuss, she held my hand and stayed close. I wished there was something I could do for her, some way I could pull her out of the shell she was building—something to distract her from her morbid fantasies of *underneath*.

A thought had been gnawing at me all morning. Annie was lonely. That's all. She had no one to belong to anymore. No one to trust. And no matter how hard I tried, I couldn't break through to her; there was a part of her she was going to keep to herself now.

Inevitably, she pulled me over to the pet store window. She always liked looking at the puppies. So did I—except while she was fussing about each little cute furry personality, I was feeling sorry for them, locked in those enclosures, those cages, like pieces of merchandise, unable to get out, unable to run and play and bark.

And always, the inevitable question, "Daddy, can we get a puppy? Puh-leeeeese? Look, this one's only sixty dollars."

I peered close. Only sixty dollars for twenty-four months. "Uh-uh, sweetheart. Not one of these."

"Why not—?"

"Um, because—" *Why not?* "—because, these aren't good watchdogs."

"Why do we need a watchdog—?"

"Because I can't sleep with you every night. We need a special kind of watchdog—a dream watchdog. A little pooch to snuggle up next to you and not let any bad dreams get in. Just like I did."

"Oh." She considered it. I could see her turning the thought over in her head. "Well, where do we get a dream watchdog?"

"Mmm, well, I dunno…." I was barely a half-step ahead of her. We had been talking about a puppy, maybe for Christmas, but what with one thing and another, including a new baby on the way—we'd decided to wait a year, until Annie was bigger. Now, however, maybe a dog was just the right thing.

"I know—let's go to the animal shelter. I'll bet they have good dream dogs there." Annie grabbed my hand and started pulling. I let myself be led back toward the parking lot. By the time we got to the car, Annie was already making plans for her pound-puppy. "I'll give him my blue blanket, okay? And he'll sleep on my bed with me, okay? And I'll call him—um, what's a good name for a dream watchdog, Daddy?"

"Well, it's been my experience that you have to live with a dog for three days, and at the end of three days, you'll know what his name is."

She nodded. "That sounds good."

The animal shelter is a depressing place. It's clean, the dogs are all well-cared for, the staff is friendly and helpful—but you know, going in, that there aren't enough homes for all these imploring hopeful faces. Only the young ones, the cute ones, the healthy ones are likely to find homes where they'll be loved. Annie limped in behind me and I realized again that she was no longer one of the cute or healthy ones. People would look at her, and then to me, and I could see the flicker of pity behind their eyes—*that poor man, having that poor disfigured child.*

The puppy cages were closest to the entrance. There weren't many to choose from. A scruffy and scraggly-looking lot. Except—

"Daddy, how about this one?"

"He's awfully small—"

"Oh, no—he's just the right size."

The card on the cage said he was a gray terrier-poodle mix, eight months old. To my eyes, he looked like he was half poodle, half opportunist; but his tail was bobbed, that indicated breeding, perhaps for show. Silvery fur, darker on top; not quite curly—kinky. He was all dreadlocks. He needed grooming. I didn't think there was very much dog inside all that fur, but he had bright attentive eyes. He watched us both, his gaze flicking back and forth between Annie and myself, then finally fixing on her as the most likely mark, he stood up, putting his paws against the bars, and tried to shove his tiny muzzle through, his tongue already licking toward Annie's fingers. She held out her hand the way I'd showed her, the back of the hand so the dog could sniff without being able to nip. He skipped the sniff, went right for the lick—this little pooch was people-friendly. More than that, he was desperate to be let out of this cage.

Without asking, I knew his backstory. It was a familiar one. This was last year's Christmas present to somebody, maybe somebody's child—and now they'd gotten tired of it, and so they discarded it, tossing it away as if it had no feelings of its own. This frantic little hairball had invested his whole being-ness into belonging to someone who couldn't be bothered to repay loyalty in kind. He had to be feeling confusion and hurt and fear. I hunched down on my knees and offered my own hand. "What do you think, little guy? Do you think you can stand guard over my Annie here and keep her safe from bad dreams?" It was an awfully big responsibility for such a little dog. He couldn't have weighed very much. Six, maybe seven pounds. I wondered if he was too small, if he'd be a yappy little nuisance; was that why he'd been abandoned to the system?

But there's this about dogs. When you look into their eyes, if all you see is a dog, then it's just a dog; but if you see a little furry person there, then he's part of your family, take him home. I wasn't sure about this guy, yet—but there was something very alive and real behind those eyes. "Do you like this one, Annie?"

"Oh, yes, Daddy. Very much." And then, she stopped herself. "Will he be a good dream dog?"

"Well—he's a terrier. And terriers are good at catching rats. So he should be a good watchdog for bad dreams. Let's go see if we can adopt him."

There was a lot of paperwork, more than I expected, and it took a while. Annie quickly grew impatient, which under other circumstances would have annoyed me, but I was secretly pleased to see her so excited, so I told her to go wait by the cage and keep her new puppy company, so he'd have a chance to get to know her. "Talk to him and let him know we're paying his bail." She didn't get the joke, but that was okay, she went anyway.

By the time I finished, Annie was sitting on the floor in front of the cage with the puppy happily curled in her lap. A thoughtful attendant had arranged it. "His name is Chester," she announced.

"Chester, huh——?" The little guy's ears pricked up and he cocked his head at me.

"See? He already knows his name. Are we done? Can we take Chester home now?"

"Sure, we can." I reached out and let the little guy sniff my hand. He licked my fingers happily. Hell, if I'd been locked up in one of these cages, I'd have licked a few fingers to be let out too.

On the way home, we stopped at the local Petco for dog food, pet bowls, a collar, a wire brush, shampoo, flea and tick treatment, a name-etag, a chew bone, a couple of small squeaky toys, a box of dog cookies, and a pet bed—a blue velvet pillow, impossibly decadent. "But he won't need his own bed, Daddy—he's going to sleep with me."

"Yes, sweetheart, but he still needs a bed of his own for his afternoon nap. Dogs like to have their own special places, just like people." The total bill was over $150 and we still weren't through. We still had to have doggie shots.

Annie spent the rest of the day showing Chester around the house and the yard, carefully explaining everything to him, "This corner of the back yard, this is where you poop. This is the kitchen, this is where we'll feed you dinner. This is my room, this is your bed here—" A blue velvet pillow, Chester dutifully sniffed it, then lay down in the center, as if to demonstrate he understood that this bed was his.

"But at nighttime, you'll sleep over here with me, Chester." Annie scooped him up and put him on her own bed. Chester repeated his performance, carefully sniffing the blanket and pillows, finally settling himself in the most comfortable place to curl up for a nap—right between Annie's two favorite stuffed toys, a pink teddy bear and a big blue bunny. "Daddy, look! Chester likes my bed."

"I'm sure. It's the nicest bed in the whole house." I was beginning to have concerns that Annie was going to smother Chester with affection, that she saw him as a toy, a living teddy bear that she could cuddle forever. But if Chester was a normal terrier, he'd set his own rules soon enough.

Very quickly, Chester revealed his own distinct personality. He didn't like to play tug of war, not even with a clean sock toy—actively disinterested. He preferred to play chase-the-squeaky. And sometimes roll-on-your-back-and-bite-the-squeaky. And most often, toss-the-squeaky-at-your-feet. When he got tired of that game, he did laps from the kitchen to the dining room to the living room, down the hall to Annie's bedroom, then back again to the living room, through the dining room, and skittering across the kitchen floor to a hairpin turn at the wash machine to do it all again. Annie laughed out loud, the first time since the accident. This had been a good decision.

Later, I tucked Annie and Chester into bed together. He snuggled in like a happy little lump. Annie petted him and whispered something in his ear, something about being a good guard dog against bad dreams. He licked her face, as if in happy agreement.

A half hour later, I peeked in at the two of them. Both were asleep, but Chester had quietly gotten down off Annie's bed and gone to his own pillow in the corner. I scooped him up—he didn't protest, he almost didn't even wake up, most puppies are that pliable—and put him down next to Annie again, a furry little comma. Still asleep, he stretched his legs out briefly, then relaxed again.

I puttered around for an hour, cleaning the kitchen, straightening up the living room, glancing into my office, wondering if I should try to get some work done, then finally, feeling like nothing in particular, I gave up. Just before heading off to my own bed, I checked in on Annie one more time. Chester was back on his velvet pillow. Once more, I scooped him up and put him down next to Annie. He trembled slightly, an odd reaction, then relaxed back into a deep sleep.

Annie woke me up, crying. "Daddy, there's something wrong with Chester!"

I glanced blearily at the clock—it was legally morning. Somewhere. I rolled out of bed with a sinking feeling and followed Annie back to her room.

Chester was lying on the bed, trembling, whimpering. When I put my hand on his side, he flinched and yelped—but he didn't lift his head. I scooped him up and held him gently in my arms—he screamed, a strange sound for such a small animal, breathless wails of panic. I slid my palm around his narrow chest, feeling for a heartbeat. It felt too fast for me, but small animals have very rapid heartbeats and I'm no vet, I had no idea if this was normal. He shivered in my grasp—not the nervous shivering that small dogs are prone to, this was something else.

Annie watched us both, wide-eyed and too afraid to speak. I continued to hold the little pooch against my chest, lowered my face to the top of his head and began whispering. "It's all right, guy. You're a good boy. Everything's all right." He stopped crying, but he continued to tremble.

"Is he going to be all right?"

"I think so. He's just scared—"

Abruptly, I remembered something from a dozen years ago—another terrier, a short-haired sweetheart named Biscuit, as tan as a perfect pancake; when she put her ears up, she looked like Anubis. She loved people, she loved to play, and she was apparently fearless. I'd take her with me on walks to the store and back. When we turned onto our block, I'd take her off the leash so she could run free all the way home. She bounced with excitement. Except one time—she hadn't gotten more than a few bounces ahead when two huge German shepherds dashed out from behind a hedge. One of them grabbed her firmly by the neck; the German shepherds were young, barely a year old, just big overgrown pups, and they had come running out to play, except they were used to playing rough and Biscuit hadn't seen them coming, she was caught by surprise. If an eagle had swept down from the sky and plucked her away, she couldn't have been more terrified. She let out a wail of panic like nothing I'd ever heard before. It turned into a series of long hurtful cries. The German shepherds backed away, startled, and I scooped up Biscuit so fast she didn't even realize it was me—she just kept on crying and trembling in panic. "All right, all right. It's okay." I looked her over carefully, her fur was ruffled, but she hadn't been bitten—just grabbed hard. I held her close and tried to comfort her all the way home, but she wouldn't let me put her down. She was terrified. And when we did get home, she ran for her bed and stayed there until the following morning.

But that had been a tangible event—Biscuit had been grabbed by a much larger, momentarily ferocious animal that had leapt out of nowhere and ambushed her. This was ... I didn't know what it was. Why was Chester crying? I'd seen dogs dreaming before, even having bad dreams—two or three short whimpers, maybe some leg motion, and then the moment was past. But this—Chester was behaving as if he'd been in a fight, grabbed and shaken and hurled against a wall.

I looked to Annie. The first question that came to mind was the one I didn't dare ask. *Did you do something, Annie?* And if I did ask it, I wouldn't get an honest answer. "Did you see anything, Annie?"

She shook her head.

"You didn't roll over on him by accident or bump him, did you?"

"Nuh-uh. He just started crying all of a sudden. He woke me up." And then she added, "Chester was having my dream. He was barking and growling at the *underneath*. But I wasn't scared, because Chester was protecting me, just like you said he would. And then—it—it—and he screamed and I woke up and he was—he was like that, and I came to get you. Is he going to be all right, Daddy?"

Chester was calming down. He'd stopped crying, stopped whimpering, and his trembling had ebbed to periodic spasms—short, intense bursts; normal for a small excitable dog, but something had freaked this animal, that was certain. I started to put him back down on the bed, but as I lowered him, he went rigid and resistant; instead, I carried him over to the corner and settled him down on his own pillow. He sat trembling, eyes wide, staring up at me.

"All right, let's get dressed. We'll take him to the doctor. He needs his shots anyway." At first, I'd wondered if perhaps Chester had been bitten by a spider or stung by a bee; but if he had, he would have gone into shock by now.

Chester didn't want to stay in Annie's room. He followed me back to my bedroom and stayed close to me while I pulled on my pants and an old sweatshirt. Then he followed me to the kitchen and stayed close underfoot while I made a fresh pot of coffee. Annie fixed herself a bowl of Cheerios, but barely touched it.

The vet's office didn't open until nine, but I knew the staff was there at seven to take care of the in-patients. I called ahead, and we pulled into the parking lot the same time as Dr. Brown. He took Chester from Annie's arms and squinted as he held him aloft. "Looks like a dog," he said. "Only smaller. Did you get him in a Happy Meal?"

Michael Brown was an old friend; we followed him inside. He put Chester on the table and listened to his heart, peeked into his ears, and even took a blood sample. He fingered Chester's bobbed tail and said, "He's probably had all his shots, but let's not take any chances. I'll give him boosters."

"But what about his bad dream—?" Annie asked.

Michael Brown looked to me. I gave him the short version. Annie added, "Chester is my dream watchdog."

"A dream watchdog, eh? Any other symptoms?"

I shook my head. "No. Just the crying and the trembling."

"Any vomiting?"

"I didn't see any."

"Diarrhea?"

"No. Nothing." A thought occurred to me. "Could it have been a seizure?"

"Not from what you describe. It sounds like he had a bad dream." Dr. Brown peered into Chester's face again, then rubbed his head affectionately. "You look fine to me."

I wasn't satisfied. "A bad dream? That bad? Can dogs have panic attacks?"

Dr. Brown shrugged. "Dunno. It was his first night in a strange place. You don't know what he might have been through before you got him. He doesn't look abused, but it's possible he heard a sound that reactivated a very bad memory. It happens to people, it happens to animals. Have you ever seen a St. Bernard scared of lightning?"

"No."

"Not a lot of fun." He handed Chester to me. "Take him home. Let him rest in a quiet dark corner. Keep an eye on him. Call me if anything changes, but he should be all right."

Logically, I knew there had to be a rational explanation for all of this. But the sequence of illogical events argued for a more compelling and mysterious pattern—and whether there was logic or not was ultimately irrelevant, because Annie believed in the logic of her dreams.

And so did I. In the cold yellow light of the afternoon, all bad dreams seem silly. But I could still feel the troubled resonance of my own downward journey. I spent the afternoon prowling through my files on phobias, panic attacks, unreasonable fears—and successful counter-therapies as well. There wasn't much here that I didn't already know. Most of it boiled down to "don't invest any more energy into the fear, that only makes it larger."

That meant no more dream catchers, magic spells, or even dream watchdogs. We had to invest our energies into something positive and joyous. Except—that was the problem. I had a little girl without a mommy, with a scar and a limp; a little girl who had lost her joy somewhere between Highway Twelve and the intensive care unit. There was no joy anymore, because Mommy never woke up.

What there was, was the slow steady, step-by-step, plodding through the process of "learning to live with it." How do I explain to her that the pain never goes away, it just becomes another part of you. You end up adding it to the mosaic of your life, a particularly hard-colored moment that you spend as little time as possible dwelling on. When you're six years old, how do you learn to do that?

By afternoon, Chester was ready to play again, as if nothing bad had happened last night. Annie spent the early hours of the evening tossing the squeaky toy for him. She even started calling him "doodle-bug" because of the way he doodled the toy around before finally giving it back. He punched the little red ball with his nose, tossing it toward her, obviously inviting her to pick it up and throw it for him. Annie laughed exuberantly, held the toy high, then hurled it down the hall. Chester bounced after it.

When bedtime finally rolled around, both Annie and her little doodle-bug trotted off obediently. Annie limped. Chester trotted, with the squeaky still in his mouth.

The little gray dog settled himself on his pillow, the red ball between his paws, and adamantly refused to get back up on Annie's bed. Every time I lifted him up and put him next to Annie, he promptly jumped right back down to the floor and went back to his own place. Annie tried calling him and patting the bed next to her, but he just curled up and ignored her. Her crestfallen expression said it all.

"Maybe he's still feeling bad from this morning. It's all right, sweetheart. I'll stay with you." I tucked her in, then I kicked off my shoes and lay down next to her. After a moment, I got up, scooped up Chester and put him between us. I put a hand on his back, not to hold him down, just to reassure him. He looked at me for a moment, then put his head between his paws. He looked sad. Or resigned.

Annie drifted off to sleep quickly. I thought about getting up and tiptoeing out, but the instant my breathing shifted, Chester's head came up. His little button nose sniffed the air, his eyes weren't visible in the darkness, but I could feel a sudden tenseness in his posture. He growled—it wasn't much, but then he wasn't much of a dog; just a little bit of meat and bone, and the rest was dust-bunny and attitude. His growl was so high-pitched, it was almost a cartoon—but he was serious. I remembered an old saying; it's not the size of the dog in the fight that counts, it's the size of the fight in the dog.

"It's all right, mini-pooch," I said, patting his flank. "There's nothing there." His growl faded. After a bit, he put his head down again. Resting, not sleeping. Every so often, his head would come back up, as if he were staring at something on the other side of the wall. He'd watch the unseen threat for a bit, then lower his head again. Occasionally, he'd mutter a soft meaningful "werf."

I woke up a couple of hours later. I didn't know why. Just a sudden awareness. Annie was sleeping soundly next to me. Chester lay between us, stretched out comfortably. Whatever threat he'd imagined, either it was gone or he was too tired. I got up and headed to the bathroom. I checked all the doors and windows, made sure all the lights and all the appliances were turned off, then headed back to Annie's room. Everything was all right there as well. So I padded off to my own bed. Maybe we were finally over the hump. Maybe.

Just before dawn—I was halfway down the hall before I realized I was awake, responding to an unearthly scream. Too high-pitched to be Annie's voice—but it was. Or maybe it was her scream dissolving into the tail-end of whatever had screamed first.

The light from the hallway shone a bar of brightness into her room. Annie had leapt backwards out of bed, trembling in her nightgown, backed against the wall. Her bed was askew as if something big had picked it up and thrown it sideways, the sheets and blankets ripped and disheveled, and toys and books and clothes torn from her closets and drawers and shelves were everywhere. Annie pointed, still gasping—

"Where's Chester?" I didn't wait for an answer. I pulled back the blankets. The little dog lay limp on her bed—at first I thought he was dead, but his heart was beating rapidly. His breath was shallow; with my hand on his side, I could barely feel any motion. He looked shredded; he was covered with dozens of tiny bites. I peeled back his upper lip; his gums were pale, he was in shock.

Annie's face was crumpled in terror; she was half-crying, half-screaming. I grabbed her and held her. I didn't even try to ask what happened, I just scooped her up and held her. With one hand, I fumbled for the flashlight, then cursed and gave up. I flicked the light switch. Still carrying Annie, I turned on all the lights. There was nothing there. Nothing anywhere. I spotted the flashlight where I'd left it the night before and grabbed it. I could use it as a club, if I had to. I looked under her bed, in the closet, checked the windows, then went back to Annie, ran my hands up and down her sides, her arms, checked her head; she seemed unhurt.

Turned back to Chester—

"Is he going to be all right?"

"I don't know. Put on your clothes. We'll take him to the doctor." I checked again to see if he was still breathing. He was very still. I pulled on my pants and a sweatshirt, grabbed the car keys and my phone. I lifted Chester carefully, cradling him in one arm; with the other hand, I punched for Dr. Brown. Annie was pulling on her bathrobe and limp-hobbling toward the door to the garage.

Michael Brown met us at the back door of the clinic.

"I'm sorry for waking you—"

He ignored it. "Come on in the back—"

We followed him in. He switched on lights as he went. "Put him there—" A cold stainless steel table. He opened a cupboard and began pulling things out. Syringes, tiny bottles, a surgical kit. "Annie, go stand over there. I want you out of the way. You, over here." He switched on a bright overhead light. He peeled back Chester's eyelids, peeled his upper lip and looked at his gums, even lifted up what was left of the little guy's tail and examined his rectum—to see if the muscles were still tight. He plugged a stethoscope into his ears and listened to Chester's heartbeat and breathing with a grim expression. At last, he grabbed syringe and a bottle of adrenalin. A quick injection directly into the heart. He listened again with the stethoscope, frowning.

Abruptly, he pasted three electrodes onto Chester's little gray chest. He switched on a monitor and the machine next to it and grabbed the defibrillator paddles—smaller versions than the ones on television. The monitor showed a very shallow, very uneven heartbeat. Dr. Brown applied the paddles; there was a short sharp sound and Chester jerked. Then he lay still again. A second shock, still no change.

"Daddy—?"

"Sometimes it takes a couple of tries, sweetheart."

"Take her out of here," Michael said.

I scooped her up and we went out into the waiting room. I sat down on the bench and held Annie in my lap.

"He's going to die, isn't he?"

"I don't know, sweetheart. I don't know."

"He doesn't deserve to die. He saved me."

"Saved you?"

"From…it."

I didn't know what to say, so I said nothing.

"He saved me," she repeated.

"Yes, he did," I agreed.

"He's a good dream watchdog."

"Yes, he is."

"He didn't let…*it*…get to me."

"No, he didn't."

We sat for a while in silence. Waiting. Annie leaned her head against my chest and was very still. I wondered if she'd fallen back asleep, but I wasn't going to shift my position to see. When Michael Brown came out of the back, she was instantly awake again. Michael looked grim. He shook his head without saying anything.

"What was it—?" I started to ask, but his expression was guarded; he wasn't going to discuss the details in front of Annie.

"He's dead," she said. "Isn't he?"

"I'm sorry, sweetheart." Dr. Brown went down on one knee so he could look her directly in the eye. "I did everything I could."

"I know," she answered calmly. Then she looked up at me. "Daddy?" she said. "We're going to need a bigger dog."

SALES OF A DEATHMAN

"Whatever else people say about this job, it's a necessary part of society. It's work that needs to be done."

Justin scratched his head, rubbed his nose, and shifted uncomfortably in his chair. "Yes, I know all that. I mean, the job counselor explained it. More than once. She said I had an aptitude. That's why she sent me here. She said I was good with people. People like me. People trust me. At least, that's what she said."

"Yes, that's all here in your file." The woman behind the desk had an oddly dispassionate way of speaking. Soft-looking, quiet and managerial, she glanced through the file, turning pages slowly. "Actually, she said that you present yourself as unintrusive and non-threatening. That's what makes you perfect for this job."

Justin nodded politely. "I suppose that's supposed to be a compliment."

"It is. You have no idea how many people come to us with the wrong idea about what we do here. Or simply the wrong attitude. People motivated by fear, anger, jealousy, revenge, or even the vain hope that this is a way to cheat the system. It isn't. It's about service. We provide a service necessary to the maintenance of our technological society."

"Yes, that's what the orientation video said."

She closed the file. "What we're looking for are people who can submerge themselves so completely in the job that they disappear. All that's left is the service. Maybe you're up to it, maybe you aren't. There's only one way to find out. What do you think?"

"I don't know. Are you trying to talk me out of it?"

"Let me be candid," she said. "The job does take an emotional toll. It requires a level of inner stamina that most of our applicants are incapable of maintaining for very long. That's why we have a probation period. That's true of any job, of course, but here your probation period is indefinite."

Justin took a deep breath. "I live with my dad. He's not the easiest person in the world to live with, but he needs me. So I take care of him. I've done it for eleven years now. I had to quit school, but he's my dad. I think that proves something. I mean, about my ability to be strong inside."

She nodded without expression. "Yes, we'll see. Do you have any other questions?"

Justin started to shake his head, then stopped. "Um. How are the health benefits?"

*

The old man sat alone in his wheelchair, staring out the window, staring down at the street below, the torn awning of the second-hand shop, the sign-plastered window of the liquor store, the groaning bus that farted black smoke as it rumbled past. The same view every day, the same people, hurrying, hunched over, caught in the desperate struggle to keep up with their own lives. The old man grunted and pushed his wheelchair backward away from the window.

In the corner, a television set babbled soundlessly. Eleven minutes of shallow people pretending to be concerned, then four minutes of even shallower people explaining all the different ways a person could smell bad. Lather, rinse, repeat four times an hour. "Pfeh." He turned away from it, facing the front door instead.

At last, he heard the sound of a key in the upper deadbolt, the second deadbolt, and finally the bottom one. Justin pushed his way in, carrying two grocery bags. "I bought a chicken for dinner, dad. Roast chicken, just the way you like it. To celebrate."

"You're late. I need to pee. You want me to piss my pants again?"

"It's only five." Justin put the bags on the kitchen table and came back to his father. He bent and kissed the old man's forehead, then went around to the back of the chair to push him to the bathroom. "Come on, let's get you taken care of, and then I'll start dinner. I bought a roast chicken at the market. Your favorite. To celebrate."

"I'm not in the mood for chicken. Chicken is Sunday. Why were you late? Why didn't you call? Help me onto the toilet."

"I went for a job interview. And that's why we're having chicken."

"You got a job? You can't get a job. Who's going to take care of me?"

"I'll still be here. It's a service job. I can set my own hours. And I haven't accepted yet."

"What kind of a job is it?"

"It's a very good one. It's for the Department of Enabled Actuarial Transitional Health. I could make enough money I could even hire a part time nurse for you, if you want."

"I don't want a nurse. And what's the Department of whatever you said anyway? What are you going to do for them? Stare at a screen all day? You already do that here. I'm done. You can help me off the toilet now. I can pull up my own pants. I'm not a baby."

"Yes, dad. Let me wash my hands now and I'll start dinner."

Justin wheeled his father into the apartment's tiny kitchen. It would make the preparation of dinner a little more difficult, but it was easier than listening to complaints from the other room, always punctuated with calls of, "What? What'd you say? I can't hear you!"

Justin cut slices of chicken, cut them into chewable pieces, placed them carefully on his father's plate. Rice and peas and salad. A glass of iced tea for each.

They ate in silence, the old man chewing each piece of chicken slowly and carefully because his teeth hurt. Finally, he said, "'Course, on the other hand, if you had a job, you wouldn't be underfoot all day, annoying the hell out of me with your constant complaining."

"Yes, you'd have some quiet time for yourself."

"Hmpf. Like I need that. Nobody ever comes to visit anyway."

"You could go down to the park."

"It's not safe. I'd rather stay here." He peered across the table. "What kind of a job is it?"

"The Department of Enabled Actuarial Transitional Health. I'd be a—a field worker. A service provider."

"Service provider? What's that mean."

"If I take the job. I'd be a—a deathman. But I'm not sure I'm going to take the job."

"A deathman. Hah. Everybody thinks about it. But nobody ever wants to actually do it. Serve death? Uh-uh. Scares the screaming hell out of them. But it's still gotta be done. Like collecting garbage or cleaning sewers. Society breaks down if nobody does it." The old man grumbled. "At least it's clean work. You wouldn't come home stinking of garbage or shit."

"No, I guess I wouldn't."

"They pay good?"

"$1250 per service, to start—plus expenses, if any, like transportation. I can set my own hours. If I get assigned to a major facility, I can make several thousand dollars a day."

"That's a lot of money."

"Death isn't cheap, dad."

"'Course money isn't worth anything if you don't have your health."

"You're right about that."

"You gonna take the job?"

"I don't know. I have to go back on Monday."

"This thing about death. They say it's a public service. Cleaning up the sick and old and useless. Because they're a drain on the public body. Parasites. You're helping society. Making the world a better place. Make more room for the real people."

The old man paused to pick apart a stringy piece of chicken with his fingers. "When I was your age . . . except your mom didn't want me to. Might have done it anyway, except you came along. But I looked into it, I did. Lots of us did. Easy work, easy money." He popped the meat into his mouth and chewed for a bit. "Takes a special somethin' though. You gotta feel for people, like you're doin' them a service, helpin' them along. Otherwise, y'know, y'start to feel bad about yourself. Whatever. If you have the backbone for it, it's good work. Nobody ever gives you shit. That's for sure."

Justin stopped. He laid his fork down next to his plate. And considered carefully what his father had just said.

"Do you want me to take the job?"

"Ahh, you'll do what you want to do. You always do. You never listened to me in the past, why would you listen to me now?"

"I want your opinion. Your advice."

"My advice? Hah. Make up your own mind. I wish I had. If I had, you wouldn't be here nagging the hell out of me."

*

"It's really very simple," the training supervisor said. "You get a gray suit, a gray car, gray gloves. You go in, you lay your hands on them, they transition peacefully and without pain. That's really all that's required. And if that's all you ever did, you'd be earning your salary.

"But the good caseworkers, they make the service personal. They respect their clients, they sit with them and chat for a bit. They take the time to know them, learn something about who they are and how they lived and what makes their lives special and worth remembering. If you can see them as real people, then you can give them their transition as a gift of release. Some agents just go in and out, wham-bam-thank-you-ma'am. But the great agents take the time to make sure the client is ready to go. Every case is different. Your job, your real job, is to be a generous listener. In a sense, you have to fall in love with each client, look for the love in their hearts and the dignity in their eyes. Give them peace in their soul and you can feel good about giving them an easy and painless release."

Justin nodded slowly, hearing the words but not yet understanding the depth of meaning. All of the words, they were starting to blur together like so much jargon. In butt-simple language, the deathman kills people. He takes lives. He does it legally. As a service of a benevolent society. He does it with a transition warrant, signed by a panel of three judges who have reviewed the life-quality of the client and determined that it has depreciated beyond recovery. More jargon.

It's still death.

"Yes," agreed the training supervisor, even before Justin could finish speaking it aloud. "Everybody has that conversation. *That* one. The one about morality and conscience and isn't this a mortal sin? No, it isn't. We'd be merciful to a horse with a broken leg or a dog with distemper, wouldn't we? Why would we want to deny such a generous mercy to our loved ones? When you can achieve that level of understanding, then you can see your job as what it truly is—a service."

"I understand what you're saying," Justin replied. "It's going to take me a while to actually experience it that way."

"Don't worry. You will. Eventually. If you stick with it."

*

The hospital smelled of disinfectant and flowers and air freshener. The lights were too bright. His footsteps sounded heavy on the floor, as if his shoes were soled with granite. Maybe it was the way that people turned to look at him, then turned hastily away.

A crisp gray suit, shiny gray shoes, a pair of silent gray gloves. Except he wasn't wearing the gloves yet. Not yet. Not until the client was ready. But they still recognized him, still knew why he was here.

Justin felt uneasy, he hoped it didn't show. Could they tell that this was his first case, his first time? His face flushed with embarrassment. He bit his lips tightly together and hoped it looked like determination.

Room 223. Mrs. Bellini.

He had to ask at the nurse's station. The male nurse barely glanced up. "You should have been here a week ago. We need the bed."

"Paperwork," mumbled Justin.

The nurse jerked a thumb over his shoulder. "Back there." He punched a button on his phone. "Yeah, I've got a code gray. I'll need a DC and a gurney in five. No, make it ten. The gray's a noob."

Justin followed the general direction, found the room, and gently pushed the door open. "Mrs. Bellini?"

She didn't answer. She was a small still form beneath a pale blanket. Her skin was sallow. She had an IV in her left arm. What was left of her hair hung down in yellow strings. She was intubated and her breath rasped painfully. Her yellow eyes were open, staring blankly at the ceiling.

"Mrs. Bellini?" Justin moved into her field of view. Her eyes flicked sideways, then drifted away. "Mrs. Bellini, do you know who I am? Do you know why I'm here?"

No answer.

"My name is Justin. I'm here to ease your transition."

She lifted her right hand as if to wave him away. He stepped back. The hand fluttered helplessly in the air, like an injured bird. It had a life of its own.

Justin glanced around, grabbed a chair and pulled it close. He sat down and leaned forward. Because he didn't know what else to do, he reached out and took her hand. Her bony fingers wrapped tightly around his.

"Do you know why I'm here?"

She blinked. Once, twice. She moved her head, almost a nod. "That's good, yes."

He started to say, "Is there anything I can do for you—" then stopped himself. She couldn't speak. She didn't have the physical strength to write a note. He couldn't even offer her a sip of water. She was helpless beneath the tubes and wires.

"All right," he said. "This won't take long." He reached into the inside pocket of his coat and pulled out his gray gloves.

Her eyes widened as she watched. Justin hesitated, he stopped fumbling with the gloves and just met her gaze. He watched as her eyes filled with tears. Finally, he said, "It's time to go, sweetheart." He finished pulling on the gloves. They felt cold and smooth, they tingled. He closed his eyes and issued a wordless prayer to himself for strength, then reached over and took her hand again, pressing it between both of his. He held it for a long time, waiting and listening to the sound of her breath leaving her body for the last time.

*

The first few weeks, most of his clients were like Mrs. Bellini. A few could talk. Some of them said, "Bless you," or "Thank you." One old man called him something in Italian. Justin wasn't sure if it was a good thing or not.

A nine-year-old girl, only a few wispy strands of hair left on her head—her sunken eyes never left him. In a voice like the rustle of parchment she asked if it would hurt. "No," Justin promised. "It will be just like going to sleep."

"Will I go to heaven?"

The question startled him. "What do you think?"

"I took my sister's doll and broke it. Isn't that a sin?"

"Did you apologize to her?"

"Yes. But I didn't mean it. Daddy made me."

"Are you sorry now?"

"Yes, please. I don't want to go to hell."

"Well, I'm pretty sure that God doesn't send little girls to hell. Especially not someone as sweet and honest as you."

That seemed to satisfy her. "Okay," she said quietly, and a moment later, "I'm ready."

Justin stepped out of the way, so mom and dad could hug their little girl one more time. He used the moment to pull on his gray gloves, still so cold and smooth. When the parents finally moved away from the bed, he sat down. "Okay, close your eyes," he whispered. "And now you count to three with me, and on three, you let go. Okay?"

On three, he took her hand in his.

*

On Thursday, Justin was sent to a small house in the suburbs, where a teenager had overdosed on drugs. The paramedics were just sliding the gurney into the back of the ambulance when he arrived. They looked at him, annoyed. Justin held up the transition warrant.

"He's just a kid."

"He's had his three strikes. He's out." Justin regretted the words even before he finished saying them.

"You don't believe in rehab?"

"I do, yes. But apparently this boy doesn't." He offered the warrant for their inspection.

Neither of the paramedics reached for it. One of them said, "We've seen that paperwork before. We know."

The other added, "We also know that in cases like this, you have the right to make an onsite adjudication."

The first one said, "But you don't get paid if you don't serve, do you?"

The second one nodded over Justin's shoulder. "That's his mom, over there. She's the one who called it in."

Justin looked. A worried-looking woman, clutching her sweater close to her. He turned back to the paramedics. "I can let him go. But you know we'll all be back here again in a week. Or a month."

"Or maybe not. Maybe when he finds out that a deathman let him live, just this one more time, maybe he'll straighten out. It's your call, of course. It's your conscience."

Justin put the gloves away, back into his inside coat pocket. He couldn't think of anything else to say, so he just turned and walked back to his car. The gray car.

*

Friday morning, Justin went to see his supervisor. He knocked politely on her door, waited for her to say, "Enter," then stepped quietly into the room.

Without looking up from the screen she was studying, she waved him to a chair. After a moment, she finished and turned to him. "Problem?"

"No. Yes. Maybe. I don't know."

She glanced at her watch. "Mm hm. You're right on schedule. Three weeks. Which conversation are we going to have? The one where you tell me you can't do this anymore? Or the one where you ask for reassurance that you're doing the right thing?"

Justin flushed with embarrassment. "I guess I'm not the first person to have . . . I guess you could say, misgivings."

She laughed gently. "No. You're not the first. Which one was it? The little girl?"

"No. She was sweet. It was easy because she understood we were ending her pain. And she knew she was loved. No, it was the boy last night."

"The drug overdose?"

"Uh-huh."

"You gave him a pass."

"Yes."

"The paramedics talked you out of it?"

"And his mother was watching."

"Yes, I heard. In fact, that's why I expected you this morning. Everybody gets one of those warrants, sooner or later." She added, "You did the right thing. You erred on the side of caution. Maybe the boy will learn, maybe he won't. Probably he won't. But if there's even the slightest chance that he will, you were right to do what you did. It doesn't hurt you to be merciful. It doesn't hurt us."

She took a deep breath. "But sometimes, it does hurt the client. Sometimes in our eagerness to be the nice guy, sometimes all we do is extend the pain, stretch it out a little longer than it needs to be. It's a judgment call, and I promise you, I'll always stand behind you, no matter what you decide in such a case. As far as I'm concerned, you're a deathman, you don't make mistakes. But just be aware—sometimes, in some cases, it happens that being merciful isn't the most merciful thing you can do. Do you understand what I'm saying?"

Justin nodded. "I was thinking about his mother. I didn't sleep very well last night. If I had . . . exercised the transition warrant, the boy would be out of his pain. And so would the mom. I mean, yes, she'd have to deal with her grief for a while, but the warrant would have released her from the trap she was in. This way, he goes to the hospital, the clinic, the rehab center, he begins the cycle all over again, one more time—and the mom, she has to go through the whole cycle again too. Until the next time she finds him on the floor choking on his vomit. I could have spared her that pain. How many weeks or months or even years?"

Justin's supervisor nodded. "What you just said—that's true compassion."

"It's in the training. I paid attention."

"Yes, you did."

"I get it now. It's not just about the client. It's about the client's family—releasing them from their burdens too. That's what I'm upset about. I'm not sure I did that woman any favor."

"No, you probably didn't. Oh, if you were to ask her, she'd say you did, and she'd be enormously grateful. But in actuality, no. Her quality of life will not improve as long as she is carrying the burden of that boy and his addiction. No, Justin, you didn't do anything wrong last night. It's a lesson we all have to learn. Mercy isn't always nice. Sometimes mercy is ruthless."

She sighed, not in exhaustion but in sympathy. "Do you need to take some personal time?"

Justin shook his head. "I'm fine. I think."

"If you want to take the rest of the day, or even a couple of days, go ahead."

"Thank you," Justin said, rising. "I, uh—I think maybe I should. Thank you."

On the way out, Justin ran into the dispatch officer. He was holding a fresh warrant.

"Um, no, I probably shouldn't. I'm supposed to take a personal day."

"Sure, okay. No problem. I was just thinking convenience."

Justin rubbed his nose. "Okay." He took the transition warrant and shoved it into his coat pocket without looking at it. "I can take care of it tonight."

"Or tomorrow," said the officer. "Whenever it's convenient. The client isn't going anywhere."

*

In the morning, Justin helped his father out of bed and into the bathroom. He sat him down on the plastic chair in the shower and helped him bathe, using a shower head on a flexible hose so the old man wouldn't have to twist or turn more than necessary.

After he dressed his father, he lifted him into the wheelchair and rolled him into the kitchen. "Would you like some bacon and eggs this morning, dad?"

"Too expensive. Why are you spending all this money? Oatmeal."

"We can afford it now. Remember, I have a job."

"Eggs and bacon. Cholesterol and fat. Trying to kill me, are you?"

"No, dad. I'm trying to make you happy. Sunny side up? Or scrambled?"

"Scrambled. Hmpf."

"And what channel would you like today? History or Animals or National Geographic?"

"Doesn't matter, they're all the same. And don't get so uppity. I know how to use the remote."

"Yes, you do know. It's right there for you."

"Don't you have to go to work already?"

"Not today. I'm taking a personal day."

"They fired you already?"

"No, dad. They said I did good. They just want me to have some time to—to think about how some things. It's part of the job."

"Hmpf. I know what happens when you start thinking. You tie your-self in a knot. You get all stuck. Well, don't you do that now. You have a good job. It keeps us in bacon and eggs. Don't you give up now. What? No toast?"

"It's in the toaster, just a minute more. And no, I'm not giving up my job. I'm just—sorting some things out."

"Sorting? Hah. Nothing to sort. Just do it. Don't be a damn wussy."

While his father sorted through his breakfast, complaining his way through the meal, Justin busied himself with little things. Washing the pan, putting away the bread, pouring himself a cup of coffee. His gray coat was on the back of his chair, he picked it up and started for the closet, then remembered the unfulfilled warrant in the pocket.

The warrant had a blue stripe across the top. He'd never gotten one of those before. It meant 'Optional.' To be exercised at the discretion of the server. Another judgment call.

Actually, it was an acknowledgment. This is how much we trust you now.

He didn't open it, he just tapped it against his fist for a moment, thinking. Remembering his orientation, remembering his training. Remembering what his supervisor had said. "You're not just releasing the client, you're releasing the family as well."

Maybe she'd said it to make this kind of decision easier, but in Jason's mind, no—it only complicated the matter. Who was he really serving?

But he already knew the answer to that one too. Again, from his training. Step back from the immediate circumstances. You're serving everyone. Figure out where the real service is and you'll know what to do.

He shook away the thought. In theory, it was an easy conversation. In practice, it wasn't about conversation. He unfolded the warrant without looking at it. Okay. If nothing else, it would get him out of the apartment for a bit. Maybe some fresh air, a walk through the park, a chance to sit and not think.

The old man wheeled himself into the living room. "You're doing it, boy, aren't you? Thinking yourself into a corner."

"No, dad. I'm not thinking at all."

"Well, then why don't you do something useful. Go to work. Make some more money."

"Yes, that's probably a good idea." He glanced down at the paper in his hand. He wasn't surprised. He'd been expecting it. All the myriad little conversations fluttered around him for a moment, then evaporated. He understood.

He understood everything.

He reached into his inside coat pocket.

He began pulling on his gloves.

"Dad? Have I told you today how much I love you?"

NIGHT TRAIN TO PARIS

How I ended up in Milan takes some explanation.

I'd been invited to speak to a science-fiction media convention in Bellaria, a small resort town halfway up the eastern side of the Italian boot. I assumed the audience enjoyed what I had to say, but afterward the English translation of the web review said that I "totally fell" and that I was "less brilliant." I decided not to let it bother me. It was probably true and I've been called worse in English.

I wandered around Italy for a bit, finally ending up in Venice—a clustered jumble of narrow passages, shops, canals, bridges, piazzas, and little shops filled with gaudy glassware or glittering masks, plus pastries and pizza everywhere. The whole thing is a puzzle box, a gaudy architectural confection too preposterous to be real, crowded with herds of gray-haired tourists (of which I was now one) and people taking pictures of each other. After three days, I was ready to move on. I planned to spend a few days in Paris, then London where I had some business waiting for me.

The usual way from Italy to Paris is through Geneva, but I'd done that trip. I wanted to see some different countryside. Looking at a map, I assumed I could catch a train from Milan to the south of France, famous among impressionist painters for its wonderful light, so I booked a morning reservation and arrived in Milan shortly after noon. That's when the "adventure" began.

Trenitalia didn't have any trains to the south of France. Not from Milan. They did have one to Geneva, where I could catch a train to Paris, but it had already pulled out. The only train to France was the night train to Paris, leaving at 23:38. But they wouldn't honor my rail pass, 96 euros please. I dithered with the lady at the customer service desk for a bit, trying to find an alternate way out of Italy, but there wasn't one.

My options were simple. Stay in Milan for a night so I could catch the next day's train to Geneva and then Paris—and lose another whole day in travel—or spend the 96 euros and take the night train to Paris. Thinking about it, the cost of the train would be almost the same as a hotel room, maybe a little more, and I'd be in Paris at 9:09 the next morning. Of course, it also meant an eight-hour layover until the train boarded.

I thought a short walk through the neighborhoods surrounding the train station might use up some time, but I found little to hold my interest. I did find a McDonalds with free wifi, but I've never had much interest in pictures of cats with badly-spelled captions. Back at the terminal, I still had six hours to wait. I found a place to sit at the end of a long row of chairs and curled up with the first book of a popular seven-book trilogy (of which, only the first five have been published—starting an unfinished series was an act of faith on my part, an assumption that someday there would be a conclusion.) The television adaptation had caught my interest enough that I had grown particularly impatient to see a certain little weasel receive a well-deserved and extremely painful death. The rhythm of the tale demanded it.

I confess, I do not read many works of pseudo-medieval fantasy. My mind starts wandering into questions of physicality. Nobody wakes up the morning after a battle, aching and bruised, in too much pain to move. Nobody's wounds get infected. Despite the absence of hot baths, everybody is leaping eagerly into bed with everybody else, and nobody ever catches a sexually-transmitted disease. You never hear about the fleas and the lice either. Or the pox.

Shortly, I discovered why you cannot read for long in a train station—especially not a European train station. The ever-changing multitudes passing through are a magnet for pickpockets and beggars. My best defense against a pickpocket is to wear an angry scowl and a photographer's vest with a multitude of zippered compartments. So far, that's worked—but there is no equally effective defense against panhandlers.

In my imagination, the Milanese beggars have organized themselves into some kind of Mendicants Guild, all working the same route through the train station, spacing themselves at five minute intervals. First the stoop-shouldered old woman in a shawl, a few minutes later the tall black man with a thick unrecognizable accent, and after him a frantic-looking woman of disheveled appearance, a little later the scraggly old man without any teeth who reeks offensively of alcohol and urine, then of course, a young woman with an adorable but forlorn toddler in hand—and finally, the aggressive fat woman who confronts with such a demanding demeanor the only possible response is rudeness. She strides away as if you're the one in the wrong.

One at a time, they start at the south end of the row of chairs and work their way up. Reaching the last seat north, they move into the main part of the terminal and continue a circuitous route through the arriving and departing passengers, eventually coming back around full circle to the south end of the line of chairs again.

If you're only waiting for a short time, you don't see the pattern. If you're sitting for more than an hour, you start to recognize the players in this game. I began to feel like a character trapped in a Charles Dickens novel. Perhaps I could have one of those wonderfully unforgettable names—Fetcher Pennysworth or Carfax Abbey, something like that. But here in the Milan train station, any sustained mental exercise—working on the laptop, reading, or just listening to music—slowly goes from uncomfortable to impossible. The interruptions come one after another. It's not just Milan, of course. All the major train stations in Europe have the same entourage of scroungers, vagabonds, and opportunists. They've been here since before Caesar. They'll probably be here accosting travelers when we're all beaming from place to place via public teleportation portals. The passengers will arrive and depart, the beggars will stay, the only permanent residents of the terminal.

At last, with little time to spare before departure, the giant display board announced that the night train to Paris would be leaving from Bin 14. I presume the same scene happens every night. Seemingly from nowhere, a crowd coalesces into a surge, everyone hurrying down the platform with worried expressions and too much luggage. Myself included. I followed the flow, getting quickly caught up in it, one more pebble in a horizontal avalanche.

My ticket assigned me to Carriage 89, almost all the way up to the front of the train. It was a long walk and my legs had already begun to remind me with appropriate twinges and pains that I am no longer a young man. Out of breath and aching from the effort, I arrived at the carriage, shoved my suitcase up the steps and pulled myself in after it.

My compartment was toward the front of the car. More distance to push my luggage. I had not been buying souvenirs, but my suitcase was getting heavier anyway, all across Europe. I blamed the suitcase, not my age. At last, I pushed my personal entourage into the narrow cabin and sank gratefully onto the broad seat that I expected to be my bed for the night.

Just sitting quietly by myself—no noise, no beggars, nothing else to do—I could let myself relax. Next stop, Paris. Departure in fifteen minutes.

I pulled out my camera and snapped a few photos from the train window. A worker was walking along the track stabbing trash with a pointed stick and putting it into a plastic bag. I snapped his photo. People going about the daily business of life are fascinating to me, their faces, their postures—whole stories are written in their body language. Yes, I take pictures of scenery too, but I also take pictures of the little details, the nuts and bolts of the world—window boxes, doorways, vaulted ceilings, balconies, terraces, all kinds of architectural trim. There is genuine artistry in the ordinary—all those little things we miss because we never stop to look. To my eye, a woman looking out a window at the traffic below, caught in the afternoon sunlight, can have the same sudden beauty as a Vermeer painting of a girl with a pearl earring,

With still some time before departure and nothing else to photograph, I began reviewing my photos. I'd been experimenting with auto-HDR and a third-stop over-exposure to bring out the details in dark spaces. For the most part, the experiment had worked. The details in the dark areas were visible now, the lighter areas seemed suffused with light. I'd stumbled into it by forgetting that my glasses darkened automatically in the sunlight, so I had tweaked the exposure, but the experiment was successful. The effect reminded me of the French impressionists, especially Monet's delicate perspectives. I clicked through slowly, quite pleased with myself. Some of my photos looked good enough for publication. At least to me, they did.

My solitude was short-lived. The cabin door slammed open and a stout, husky man in workman's clothes pushed in, shoving a worn-looking duffel before him. He smelled of tobacco and alcohol and sweat. Three of my least-favorite smells.

"Buongiorno!" He boomed it in thick Italian.

"Buongiorno," I echoed, half-heartedly.

"Ahh, English!" he said. "You are English?"

"No, sorry."

"Canadian?"

"American."

"Ahh, America. I love American food. Hamburger. Cheeseburger. Barbecue, *si*? You are enjoying Italia, I hope."

"It's very beautiful," I said politely. *"Molto bella."* I'd picked up a few words and phrases, enough to say please and thank you appropriately.

The man busied himself with his luggage for a bit, pushing and shoving it into an overhead space. Meanwhile, the train lurched into action. It grumbled its way through the train yard, out of the station and into the larger brightness of the night. The shadowed lights of Milan rolled past in orange gloom. Finally, satisfied that he had stowed his luggage safely, the man settled himself opposite me, clearly ready for a conversation. "So, where in America is your home?"

"Los Angeles," I admitted.

"Ah, Los Angeles. Hollywood. Where the movie stars live. You are a movie star?"

I had to smile at that. I shook my head. Fame is not something I aspire to. Aside from a few lines of dialog in an internet episode, I've avoided the dangerous side of the camera.

"But you know the movie stars, yes?"

I shook my head again. Aside from one magic moment in Hollywood where Federico Fellini and Sophia Loren had stood next to me in the warm evening, while we waited for our respective limousines, my contact with the industry has been minimal. But I did enjoy watching her breathe. Occasionally, the gods give us little blessings to remind us that life can be amazing. But I didn't mention the episode. Some pleasures are best kept private. I was hoping he would take the hint that I had little interest in conversation this late at night.

He didn't take the hint. He thrust out his hand enthusiastically. "Claudio," he said. "I am Claudio. You are?"

I introduced myself, already resigned to the casual interrogation of a stranger in search of some common ground and the empty chatter that would inevitably follow.

He pointed to my camera. "You are photographer? A professional?"

I shook my head. I'd sold a few photos here and there, but I hadn't pursued it as an income source. Maybe someday I'd feel that my photos were worth publishing, but right now I felt certain that the National Geographic already had enough pictures of the Rialto bridge in Venice— even at 24 megapixels.

"But you take pictures, yes?"

"Yes."

"Maybe you will catch a picture of the…how do you say it? Great mystery of the train here?"

The word mystery has always caught my attention—ever since I was nine, when I'd found a copy of Edgar Allan Poe's *Tales Of Mystery And Imagination* on my father's bookshelf. Roderick Usher still lurked beneath my nightmares, a tall gaunt figure backlit by horror. But despite my relentless curiosity, I've learned to be increasingly skeptical. Most mysteries are wishful thinking.

Nevertheless, I had to ask. "This train has a mystery?"

"Si si!" he said enthusiastically. "A very great mystery. *Un grande misterioso.*" He glanced around conspiratorially. He got up, opened the cabin door, looked out—both ways—closed it, came back, sat down again. "They do not talk much of it in the public. They know what is happening, but they do not know why, so they say nothing. They pretend."

"Who doesn't say anything?"

Claudio waved his hands to indicate everything beyond the compartment in which we sat. The train was speeding up now. "All of them. The people who know."

"Uh-huh," I said. "But you know about this great mystery because?"

"Because I am Claudio and I know this thing. I ride this train many times. The *controllori*, they know me. They trust me enough to talk to me." He leaned forward and whispered. "Because they are scared."

Okay. He had me.

I leaned forward in my seat, ready to listen. "Why are they scared?"

Before he could answer, the cabin door slid open and a female conductor asked, *"Passaporti?"* I handed mine over. Claudio dug around for his, one pocket after the other, finally found it, passed it across. The conductor said, *"Grazie,"* closed the door, and disappeared.

I turned back to Claudio. "Okay," I said. "Tell me now. Why are they scared."

Something had changed his mood. He looked anxious. *"Signore,* I should not."

"Now, that's not fair. First you bring it up—then you say you can't talk about it?"

"Sometimes, too much I talk." He gestured with both hands as if wiping the conversational slate clean. "Please, we talk about something else instead."

"I don't think so. I want to know about the great mystery."

Claudio shook his head. He was adamant. "Someone else will have to tell you."

"Okay, fine," I said. The train rocked unevenly. It was getting late. I stood up and began fussing with the back of the seat, trying to lower it and turn it into a bed. "Don't tell me. Keep your secret. I am going to sleep now." I had already made up my mind to see what Google could tell me tomorrow.

"I don't think you should sleep on the train," Claudio said. "It is not a good idea."

"It's not?"

"Not on this train, I think."

"And this is because?"

He didn't answer.

"Because of the great mystery you're not going to tell me about."

"Si, si." He said it with enormous resignation.

"Okay, so I can't sleep and you won't tell me why. Thank you very much. *Grazie."* I went back to fussing with the latches that held the seat back in place. Claudio made a noise of frustration, then got up to help me, but instead of helping me lower the seat he pushed it back up into place.

"Sit, please," he said.

I sat.

"What I tell you, you promise you will tell no one else?"

"I promise," I said, not meaning it at all.

He looked at me skeptically. I was probably not the first person to lie to him, and he was not the first person I had lied to. He sighed, an audible recognition that no promise was ever really a guarantee. He turned to his luggage, digging into it like a badger, and pulled out half a bottle of red wine. He unscrewed the top, drank from the bottle, then passed it across to me.

What the hell. I took a swallow. It wasn't great wine, but it wasn't bad either. I don't know enough about wine to tell. I just know if it tastes okay.

Claudio took another swig, wiped his mouth, sat back, and prepared to unburden himself. He offered me the bottle again, I waved it off, and he began. The outside world was long gone. All that remained was this island of dim light caught in the middle of a racketing lurching sea of noise and movement.

"It is about the missing people," he said. "Many missing people now. But not at the beginning. First only one or two. This train—it used to be full every night. Many people, tourists, businessmen, families, students. Sometimes fifteen hundred, two thousand people. Every cabin full. Not so, anymore. This cabin—this is a cabin for four. Where are the other two? They do not come. Not this way. They go through Geneve instead. Or they take the coach and get on a train in Marseilles or somewhere."

"Why?"

"They are scared. They hear the stories. Nobody believes the stories, but there is still a reason to fear…." He spread his hands wide. "They stay away."

"You're riding the train," I pointed out. "Do you believe the stories?"

"I believe there is something." He shook his head. "I tell you this, *signore*. People disappear from this train. That part is not a story." He took another swig from the bottle, looked at it, sloshed the remainder around, screwed the metal cap back on. He leaned forward. "It started…I don't know how long ago, but one morning the train arrives in Paris, one passenger is not aboard. Nobody knows where he gets off. He is just gone. *Poof.* The *polizia* investigate. There is nothing. There is no body, there is no evidence. There is nothing. Two thousand people get on in Milan, Nineteen hundred and ninety-nine get off in Paris."

"That's it?"

"*Si,* that's it. So after a while they assume that maybe there was a booking error or maybe the person gets off in the middle of the night somewhere. After a while, nobody cares. It is just a missing person. Then a few days later, maybe a week, another person—*poof.* Only one. This time a young lady student. A coincidence perhaps? Another investigation, another question with no answer, a mystery. And then another and another and another. Until it is once or twice a week.

"The newspapers, the television—they report the missing people. Soon the night train gets a new name. The train of mystery. The train of disappearing people. Some people laugh about it. Some think perhaps a—how you say it? A serial murderer? Maybe. Maybe something else. Who knows? So many people still take the train. If fifteen hundred people get on, if a thousand people get on—if only one disappears, then the gamble is in your favor. It is fifteen hundred, a thousand against one. You should be safe, *si?* But still, somebody is the one.

"The *polizia*, they think it is a serial murderer. They look at everybody who travels the train, they have the numbers of the *passaporti*. They can see who was on the train when the victims disappeared."

"And—?"

Claudio smiled, grinned—a very unsavory expression. His teeth were yellow and uneven. I hadn't noticed that before. "Do I look like a serial murderer?"

"I don't know," I said. "I don't know what a serial murderer looks like."

He laughed. "Okay. You are funny. But I am on list of people to investigate. So are many many others. The *polizia* have much work to do, all the checking. But as much as they check, nobody is on the train all the times when someone vanishes. Sometimes *si*, sometimes no. But nobody always *si*."

"Unless…" I stopped.

"*Signore?*"

"I watch too much television." I waved the thought away.

"No, *signore*. Say what you are thinking. *Per favore.*"

"Well, if it were a serial killer, as you say, he could be using different passports specifically to confuse the police."

"Ahh, yes, of course. If it were a serial murderer, that would be a good way to hide. If it were a serial murderer." The train lurched and rocked. Darkness rushed past. We were a flickering moment of stillness. "If it were…."

"You don't think so?"

Claudio shrugged. "I am not an expert on these things. Are you?"

"No, I am not." The way he sat, the serious expression on his face, there was much more to this that he hadn't told me yet.

"People are still disappearing?"

"*Si.*" He said it almost with resignation. "The *polizia*, they want to cancel the train. The Trenitalia people, they would lose too much money. They want more *polizia* aboard. But sometimes, it is one of the *polizia* who disappears. So now the *polizia* want to catch the murderer even more."

"How many people now?"

"One or two a week, every week, for…" He paused to count in his head. "…many months now. Six or seven months."

"And it's still going on—?"

"*Si, si.*"

"And people are still taking the train?"

"*Si.* Yes." He nodded. "Like yourself, signore, many do not know—nobody tells them, they board the train. They get to Paris, they get off, they are happy in their not knowing. Sometimes they don't get off, one or two times a week.

"Other people—they do know. They ride anyway. Some ride on a dare. It is a great sport for young people to ride the train and pretend to be brave. Whole groups of young men and young women." He shrugged. "Sometimes reporters too. They think they are smart enough to discover the mystery of the train. They bring cameras and lights and microphones. They think they will catch the mysterious killer."

"And they disappear too?"

"No. I don't think so. I think the mystery of the train is too smart."

I had to ask. "And knowing all this, you continue to ride the train?"

"Many business people, not just me—we have our business. It is too important. Maybe like me, they think they are safe. I think I am safe. If the train wanted to eat me, it would have eaten me by now, so it doesn't want me and I am safe to ride. But sometimes, even the people who think they are safe, sometimes they don't get off the train either. Nobody is safe."

"But you still ride."

"I cannot afford to go the long way around."

"And Trenitalia still sends the train out every night."

"They cannot afford not to. It is their business. It makes them money. If they lose a rider now and then, so what? The rider has already paid for the ticket. He took his chance when he got on the train. But people keep buying tickets so Trenitalia keeps selling them. Some people say Trenitalia is in league with the devil. Not me. I think that they do not care. I think the tickets are more important to them than the caring."

"And none of this scares you?"

He shook his head. He leaned forward conspiratorially. "Do you want to know my secret, *signore?*"

I nodded. I was sure he was going to tell me anyway.

"I'll tell you my secret. I stay up all night, talking." He jabbed his finger in my direction. "I find someone to talk with, someone like you who deserves to live. I stay up all night, I keep him up all night too. We talk and talk, all night long. We drink and we talk." He waved the bottle at me, reminding himself to drink again. "Sometimes it is funny, very funny. We laugh. Sometimes even we sing brave songs. But we stay awake. The mystery of the train is that it is never more than one person at a time who vanishes. So if we are sitting and talking, it does not take either of us because it cannot take both of us. *Capisce?*"

"*Si,*" I said. "I understand." I understand that as tired as I am from the long day in the Milan train station, it's going to be an even longer night. I am not going to get any sleep on this train. This man is going to keep me up until the first glow of daylight because he's so scared. Or maybe he's not scared. Maybe this is an intricate Italian practical joke and he's telling me this preposterous story as a way to entertain himself.

"It seems to me," I said cautiously, "that it would require an enormous amount of skill and preparation to make a person disappear. I don't know that much about murder, but I'm told it can be very messy and very violent, and afterward there's the problem of disposing of the evidence—"

Claudio frowned in confusion.

"Getting rid of the body," I explained.

"Ah," he said. "*Si.* There are never any bodies. There is never anything. That is the great mystery. That is why some people—many people—say it must be an evil spirit—that the train is hunted."

"You mean haunted?"

"No, *signore.*" He shook his head as if I'd insulted him. "*Il mio englese*—my English—it is not good, but it is not that bad either. I said hunted because I meant hunted. Some people believe that there is something out there in the night—" He waved uneasily toward the empty dark window. "—something that chases the train for sport. Like a cat chases a feather on a string. Sometimes it catches it for a moment. Then lets it go so it can chase it again."

I didn't know what to say to that. I fell back on safe conversational filler. "That's an interesting thought."

Claudio nodded. His expression darkened, as if he were looking at something inside himself. Finally, he whispered, "I have seen it myself." He looked across at me and his eyes were troubled. "*Signore*, it is real. I have seen it."

"You have?"

"In the morning, you will think on this, in daylight you will decide I am—how do you say *sciocco*—foolish. But I am not. You don't have to believe me, but I believe me because I have seen it and I know what I have seen." He pointed at my camera. "If I had *la macchina fotografica* like you, I would have pictures. Then you would believe."

I should have known better. I said, "Pictures can be faked."

He shook his head. "Point your camera out the window. With your own eyes, with your own *macchina*. Maybe you will see for yourself."

"It's too dark," I said. "I won't get anything but blackness."

He looked skeptical. "You have *a macchina* that big, that expensive? And it doesn't see in the dark?"

"Cameras need light to work—*la luz*—" No, that was Spanish. "*La luce*." To prove the point, I set the camera for burst mode and popped off the lens cap. I set the exposure for auto and pointed it out the window. I ran off a string of shots. One after another. The camera clattered. I unfolded the screen on the back, held the camera out for him to look. He peered closely. "Nothing. See?"

"Try again, *signore!*"

Another rattle of frames. A third, a fourth. Black frames.

Claudio sat back in his seat, convinced. "You need a better camera."

Two thousand dollars—and I need a better camera? I didn't reply.

For a while we just sat and looked at each other. The train clattered and rocked and bumped—more than I thought any train should. But Claudio did not look alarmed at the bouncing. Finally, he said, "But...I know what I saw with my eyes."

He pointed toward the window. "There is something out there. It hunts the train. Every night. Sometimes it catches something. Sometimes it does not. I can't say what it is, I don't know. But I have seen it. It is out there. It is. The *controllori* know it too. That is why they stay up all night, huddled together in their own compartment."

I shrugged. "All right."

"You believe me?"

"I see that you believe it. If, as you say, people go missing—"

"They do," he nodded sadly.

"—then yes, there is reason to fear." And as I said it, I felt my own unease finally solidifying in my chest. What had been someone else's anxious delusion had suddenly become my own concern as well. The hollow queasiness of fear is a visceral acknowledgment of the moment—and my own dilemma had suddenly crystallized. Either this man was telling the truth and I was riding a very dangerous train—or this man was delusional and I was in a much more personal danger.

I wanted to get up, get out of the cabin, stroll up and down the narrow corridor of the car. Anything to escape this moment. Maybe there was a service car with an all-night bar? But if I left this cabin, I would be alone—and if I went alone, plodding down the narrow corridors of all the cars, past all the darkened cabins, would I be putting myself in even greater danger? And if I tried to leave, then Claudio would be alone— would he panic? Would he refuse to let me leave? Would he get violent just to keep me with him?

Maybe if I pretended I wanted to take some more pictures—I could stand in the corridor outside the compartment and fiddle with exposure and aperture and shutter speed and occasionally rattle off a few frames. I could say that I was trying to validate his story. I'd still be in his sight, but at a safe remove.

I stood. I slid open the compartment door. "I'll try some more pictures," I said. "Keep the door open and watch."

"*Signore!* Please."

"I'll be right here," I said. "You can watch me."

"But you will not be able to watch me—"

"It'll be all right, I'm sure." I stepped into the corridor. He stood up and held the compartment door open, waiting like a nervous nanny. I didn't like him standing so close behind me. I considered moving down the corridor away from him, but his anxiety was palpable. I didn't dare add to it.

I allowed myself a half-step leftward, just so I could have an un-obstructed view out the window. The train clunkered on and I braced myself against the inner wall of the passage. I fiddled with auto-HDR and dynamic-range-optimization. I pushed the exposure up, I forced the ISO all the way up to where it was nothing more than raw noise. I took streams of burst mode exposures, followed by careful single-shots, and then long exposures too. There was no point in using the flash, the glass of the window would reflect back and dazzle, but I spun off another series of shots anyway. I didn't even bother looking. With the flash, they'd come out glaring. Without the flash, everything would be black, or perhaps I'd pick up my own dim reflection in the window pane.

After half an hour, maybe more, I'd exposed a couple hundred frames. There was nothing more I could think of to do. I was starting to get bored. Whatever anxiety I'd felt in the compartment, it had faded. Now my concern was my camera again. I didn't want to drain the battery. I wouldn't be able to recharge it until I got to my hotel and I liked to leave room on the memory card too, so I returned to the cabin.

"It does not always come," Claudio said. "Maybe tonight it sleeps."

I nodded. I wished I could sleep. But now I knew I wouldn't, no matter what. Claudio offered me the wine bottle again, but I waved it off.

"It is like a great white bird," he said.

"What is?" Then I realized. "Oh."

"But instead of wings like a bird, it has long bony arms with flags attached. It trails flowing ribbons of ghostly light, like ragged banners and it runs alongside the train on high bony legs like stilts. It takes great long steps, so it looks like it runs slowly alongside and as it passes, it arches its head low to peer into the windows of the train, one after the other as if it is looking for just the right one. It has a stabbing beak, *signore,* all stretched out in front, with many teeth—and dark hollows instead of eyes, like a great white skull. It floats through the night as if the train is motionless and it is the only thing moving. And it screeches like the wheels of the carriage as the train goes around a curve."

"You saw all this?"

"*Si, signore.* And worse. I saw it stab into the train and pull a poor man out. Right through the side as if it weren't there. The man struggled and cried, but the *mostro* just tilted its head back and snapped and gulped and he was gone." Claudio's face was pale. "It could have been me. *Mio dio.*" He put his face into his hands, sobbing. "That poor man. It is my fault. I thought we were safe. We talked all night. We talked for hours. I told him we were safe. I was wrong. May God forgive me."

He wept uncontrollably for a long time. I didn't know if it was fear or grief or some anguished mixture of both. Whatever horrors were churning in this man, they had been seething for a long time. And, to be honest, I found it disconcerting. I am not the kind of person who hugs others with the comforting reassurance of "There, there, it'll be all right," because the evidence of the universe is that it is *not* going to be all right. It's only going to get worse. The best you can do is endure it. So I let him weep without interfering.

Whatever he'd seen, whatever had happened, it was his personal nightmare. There was nothing I could say or do that would alleviate his pain. The most I could do was sit and be with him, so that he would know he was not alone. That's usually enough. It should be enough. For most people anyway.

But even after he stopped weeping, he stayed with his head in his hands for the longest time. As if he was afraid to look up at me, as if he did not know what to do next, as if he were fighting within himself.

I sat and waited. My camera was still in my hands. I made a show of fiddling with it, reviewing all the frames of black, something to do so he would not think I was sitting and judging him.

At last, Claudio looked up, all red-faced and puffy-eyed. "*Signore*, forgive me."

"You don't have to apologize. There's nothing to forgive."

He shook his head. "No, no. I have taken advantage of your good nature. I have imposed myself on you. You did not invite me to intrude, but I have invaded your privacy. And I have let my terror overwhelm me. I have demanded too much of you."

I shook my head. "It's all right, Claudio. The way I see it—if human beings cannot be there for each other, then *we* are the real monsters." I chose my next words carefully. "All you've been through, it must take real strength for you to ride this train night after night, week after week."

He nodded. He pulled out a dirty red handkerchief and wiped his forehead, his mouth, his nose. "*Si, si.* Sometimes it does get to me." He looked across the tiny compartment. Both of us were swaying with the rocking motion of the carriage. "You are a kind man. At first, I thought you would be like all the others. Most people, I tell them what I have seen, they do not want to hear. They tell me to leave them alone, to let them sleep. They tell me I am crazy. But, *signore*, you did me a kindness. You listened to my story. I am sorry for scaring you so badly."

"I'm not—" I started to say, then realized it would have been a lie. "It's a very disturbing story, yes."

He sighed, he sagged, the air came out of him like a deflating balloon, and he looked around as if seeing the cabin for the first time. "I think it is safe now," he said. "If you want to sleep, I will stop talking."

"Yes, I am getting tired," I admitted.

Claudio helped me pull the back of the seat down to make a bunk and I climbed into it gratefully. The train rattled and bumped, rocking me fitfully. I assumed we were somewhere in the middle of France by now. I dozed uncomfortably, never fully asleep, never really awake either. But I must have slept some because I awakened to see bright sunlight streaming in through the window of the train. I rolled onto my side to see if Claudio was awake, but he was gone, I was alone in the compartment.

For some reason, I was not alarmed. Perhaps I should have been. But maybe he had gone to the service car.

I made my way to the lavatory at the end of the car and emptied my bladder, returned to the compartment, pushed the seat back into place, and settled myself to wait for our arrival at the Gare de Lyon. According to my watch, we were still forty minutes out.

I powered up the camera and began working my way through several hundred blank exposures, examining and deleting each one in turn. Most of them were blank. The ones that had been taken with the flash were a blur of over-exposed glare.

Except for one—aimed out through the window. There was nothing visible beyond the glass, but the pane showed a dark reflection of me peering through the viewfinder of my camera—and something darker looming behind me that should have been Claudio, but wasn't.

ABOUT THE AUTHOR

David Gerrold is the author of more than fifty books and hundreds of short stories, essays, articles, and columns.

He has written scripts for over a dozen hit television series, including *Star Trek, Twilight Zone, Star Trek Animated, Sliders, Babylon 5, Land Of The Lost,* and *Tales From The Dark Side*. His most famous script is "The Trouble With Tribbles" episode of the original *Star Trek* series.

His most popular novels are *When HARLIE Was One, The Man Who Folded Himself, The Voyage Of The Star Wolf, Jumping Off The Planet,* and *The War Against The Chtorr* series.

In 1995, David Gerrold won the Hugo, Nebula, and Locus awards for *The Martian Child,* the autobiographical tale of his son's adoption. That story was also the basis for the 2007 movie *Martian Child,* starring John Cusack and Amanda Peet.

FOR MORE BOOKS AND STORIES BY DAVID GERROLD, PLEASE VISIT HTTP://WWW.GERROLD.COM.

Lightning Source UK Ltd.
Milton Keynes UK
UKOW02f1126110117

291849UK00001B/195/P

9 781939 888426